A
NOVEL
BY

Kurt Vonnegut

SLAPSTICK

OR

LONESOME
NO
MORE!

LAUREL

*Grateful acknowledgment is extended to Al Hirschfeld,
who is represented exclusively by
The Margo Felden Galleries, New York City,
for permission to reproduce the illustration
on the dedication page.*

A LAUREL BOOK
Published by
Dell Publishing
a division of
Bantam Doubleday Dell Publishing Group, Inc.
666 Fifth Avenue
New York, New York 10103

Cover design: Carin Goldberg
Cover illustration: Gene Greif

The trademark Laurel® is registered in the U.S. Patent and Trademark
Office.

The trademark Dell® is registered in the U.S. Patent and Trademark
Office.

ISBN: 0-440-18009-0

Reprinted by arrangement with Delacorte Press/Seymour Lawrence

Printed in the United States of America

Published simultaneously in Canada

August 1989

26 25 24 23 22 21 20 19 18

RAD

BY THE SAME AUTHOR:

Dedicated to the memory of
Arthur Stanley Jefferson and Norvell Hardy,
two angels of my time.

◆◆◆◆◆◆◆◆◆◆◆◆

"Call me but love, and I'll be new baptiz'd . . "

—ROMEO

Prologue

◆◆◆◆◆◆◆◆

THIS is the closest I will ever come to writing an autobiography. I have called it "Slapstick" because it is grotesque, situational poetry—like the slapstick film comedies, especially those of Laurel and Hardy, of long ago.

It is about what life *feels* like to me.

There are all these tests of my limited agility and intelligence. They go on and on.

The fundamental joke with Laurel and Hardy, it seems to me, was that they did their best with every test.

They never failed to bargain in good faith with their destinies, and were screamingly adorable and funny on that account.

◆◆◆

There was very little love in their films. There was often the situational poetry of marriage, which was something else again. It was yet another test—with comical possibilities, provided that everybody submitted to it in good faith.

Love was never at issue. And, perhaps because I was so perpetually intoxicated and instructed by Laurel and Hardy during my childhood in the Great Depression, I find it natural to discuss life without ever mentioning love.

It does not seem important to me.

What does seem important? Bargaining in good faith with destiny.

◆◆◆

I have had some experiences with love, or think I have, anyway, although the ones I have liked best could easily be described as "common decency." I treated somebody well for a little while, or maybe even for a tremendously long time, and that person treated me well in turn. Love need not have had anything to do with it.

Also: I cannot distinguish between the love I have for people and the love I have for dogs.

When a child, and not watching comedians on film or listening to comedians on the radio, I used to spend a lot of time rolling around on rugs with uncritically affectionate dogs we had.

And I still do a lot of that. The dogs become tired

and confused and embarrassed long before I do. I could go on forever.

Hi ho.

◆◆◆

One time, on his twenty-first birthday, one of my three adopted sons, who was about to leave for the Peace Corps in the Amazon Rain Forest, said to me, "You know—you've never hugged me."

So I hugged him. We hugged each other. It was very nice. It was like rolling around on a rug with a Great Dane we used to have.

◆◆◆

Love is where you find it. I think it is foolish to go looking for it, and I think it can often be poisonous.

I wish that people who are conventionally supposed to love each other would say to each other, when they fight, "Please—a little less love, and a little more common decency."

◆◆◆

My longest experience with common decency, surely, has been with my older brother, my only brother, Bernard, who is an atmospheric scientist in the State University of New York at Albany.

He is a widower, raising two young sons all by himself. He does it well. He has three grown-up sons besides.

We were given very different sorts of minds at birth. Bernard could never be a writer. I could never be a scientist. And, since we make our livings with our minds, we tend to think of them as gadgets—separate from our awarenesses, from our central selves.

◆◆◆

We have hugged each other maybe three or four times—on birthdays, very likely, and clumsily. We have never hugged in moments of grief.

◆◆◆

The minds we have been given enjoy the same sorts of jokes, at any rate—Mark Twain stuff, Laurel and Hardy stuff.

They are equally disorderly, too.

Here is an anecdote about my brother, which, with minor variations, could be told truthfully about me:

Bernard worked for the General Electric Research Laboratory in Schenectady, New York, for a while, where he discovered that silver iodide could precipitate certain sorts of clouds as snow or rain. His laboratory was a sensational mess, however, where a clumsy stranger could die in a thousand different ways, depending on where he stumbled.

The company had a safety officer who nearly swooned when he saw this jungle of deadfalls and snares and hair-trigger booby traps. He bawled out my brother.

My brother said this to him, tapping his own forehead with his fingertips: "If you think this laboratory is bad, you should see what it's like in *here.*"

And so on.

◆◆◆

I told my brother one time that whenever I did repair work around the house, I lost all my tools before I could finish the job.

"You're lucky," he said. "I always lose whatever I'm working on."

We laughed.

◆◆◆

But, because of the sorts of minds we were given at birth, and in spite of their disorderliness, Bernard and I belong to artificial extended families which allow us to claim relatives all over the world.

He is a brother to scientists everywhere. I am a brother to writers everywhere.

This is amusing and comforting to both of us. It is nice.

It is lucky, too, for human beings need all the relatives they can get—as possible donors or receivers not necessarily of love, but of common decency.

◆◆◆

When we were children in Indianapolis, Indiana, it appeared that we would always have an extended family of genuine relatives there. Our parents and grandparents, after all, had grown up there with shoals of siblings and cousins and uncles and aunts. Yes, and their relatives were all cultivated and gentle and prosperous, and spoke German and English gracefully.

◆◆◆

They were all religious skeptics, by the way.

◆◆◆

They might roam the wide world over when they were young, and often have wonderful adventures. But they were all told sooner or later that it was time for them to come home to Indianapolis, and to settle down. They invariably obeyed—because they had so many relatives there.

There were good things to inherit, too, of course—sane businesses, comfortable homes and faithful servants, growing mountains of china and crystal and silverware, reputations for honest dealing, cottages on Lake Maxinkuckee, along whose eastern shore my family once owned a village of summer homes.

◆◆◆

But the delight the family took in itself was permanently crippled, I think, by the sudden American hatred for all things German which unsheathed itself when this country entered the First World War, five years before I was born.

Children in our family were no longer taught German. Neither were they encouraged to admire German music or literature or art or science. My brother and sister and I were raised as though Germany were as foreign to us as Paraguay.

We were deprived of Europe, except for what we might learn of it at school.

We lost thousands of years in a very short time—and then tens of thousands of American dollars after that, and the summer cottages and so on.

And our family became a lot less interesting, especially to itself.

So—by the time the Great Depression and a Second World War were over, it was easy for my brother and my sister and me to wander away from Indianapolis.

And, of all the relatives we left behind, not one could think of a reason why we should come home again.

We didn't belong anywhere in particular any more. We were interchangeable parts in the American machine.

◆◆◆

Yes, and Indianapolis, which had once had a way of speaking English all its own, and jokes and legends and poets and villains and heroes all its own, and galleries for its own artists, had itself become an interchangeable part in the American machine.

It was just another someplace where automobiles lived, with a symphony orchestra and all. And a race track.

Hi ho.

◆◆◆

My brother and I still go back for funerals, of course. We went back last July for the funeral of our Uncle Alex Vonnegut, the younger brother of our late father—almost the last of our old-style relatives, of the native American patriots who did not fear God, and who had souls that were European.

He was eighty-seven years old. He was childless. He was a graduate of Harvard. He was a retired life insurance agent. He was a co-founder of the Indianapolis Chapter of Alcoholics Anonymous.

◆◆◆

His obituary in the *Indianapolis Star* said that he himself was not an alcoholic.

This denial was at least partly a nice-Nellyism from the past, I think. He used to drink, I know, although alcohol never seriously damaged his work or made him wild. And then he stopped cold. And he surely must have introduced himself at meetings of A. A. as all members must, with his name—followed by this brave confession: "I'm an alcoholic."

Yes, and the paper's genteel denial of his ever having had trouble with alcohol had the old-fashioned intent of preserving from taint all the rest of us who had the same last name.

We would all have a harder time making good Indianapolis marriages or getting good Indianapolis jobs, if it were known for certain that we had had relatives who were once drunkards, or who, like my mother and my son, had gone at least temporarily insane.

It was even a secret that my paternal grandmother died of cancer.

Think of that.

◆◆◆

At any rate, if Uncle Alex, the atheist, found himself standing before Saint Peter and the Pearly Gates after he died, I am certain he introduced himself as follows:

"My name is Alex Vonnegut. I'm an alcoholic."

Good for him.

◆◆◆

I will guess, too, that it was loneliness as much as it was a dread of alcoholic poisoning which shepherded him into A. A. As his relatives died off or wandered away, or simply became interchangeable parts in the American machine, he went looking for new brothers and sisters and nephews and nieces and uncles and aunts, and so on, which he found in A. A.

◆◆◆

When I was a child, he used to tell me what to read, and then make sure I'd read it. It used to amuse him to take me on visits to relatives I'd never known I had.

He told me one time that he had been an American spy in Baltimore during the First World War, befriending German-Americans there. His assignment was to detect enemy agents. He detected nothing, for there was nothing to detect.

He told me, too, that he was an investigator of graft in New York City for a little while—before his parents told him it was time to come home and settle down. He uncovered a scandal involving large expenditures for the maintenance of Grant's Tomb, which required very little maintenance indeed.

Hi ho.

◆◆◆

I received the news of his death over a white, push-button telephone in my house in that part of Manhattan known as "Turtle Bay." There was a philodendron nearby.

I am still not clear how I got here. There are no turtles. There is no bay.

Perhaps I am the turtle, able to live simply anywhere, even underwater for short periods, with my home on my back.

◆◆◆

So I called my brother in Albany. He was about to turn sixty. I was fifty-two.

We were certainly no spring chickens.

But Bernard still played the part of an older brother. It was he who got us our seats on Trans World Airlines and our car at the Indianapolis airport, and our double room with twin beds at a Ramada Inn.

The funeral itself, like the funerals of our parents and of so many other close relatives, was as blankly secular, as vacant of ideas about God or the afterlife, or even about Indianapolis, as our Ramada Inn.

◆◆◆

So my brother and I strapped ourselves into a jet-propelled airplane bound from New York City to Indianapolis. I sat on the aisle. Bernard took the window seat, since he was an atmospheric scientist, since clouds had so much more to say to him than they did to me.

We were both over six feet tall. We still had most of our hair, which was brown. We had identical mustaches—duplicates of our late father's mustache.

We were harmless looking. We were a couple of nice old Andy Gumps.

There was an empty seat between us, which was spooky poetry. It could have been a seat for our sister Alice, whose age was halfway between mine and Bernard's. She wasn't in that seat and on her way to her beloved Uncle Alex's funeral, for she had died among strangers in New Jersey, of cancer—at the age of forty-one.

"Soap opera!" she said to my brother and me one time, when discussing her own impending death. She would be leaving four young boys behind, without any mother.

"Slapstick," she said.

Hi ho.

◆◆◆

She spent the last day of her life in a hospital. The doctors and nurses said she could smoke and drink as

11

much as she pleased, and eat whatever she pleased.

My brother and I paid her a call. It was hard for her to breathe. She had been as tall as we were at one time, which was very embarrassing to her, since she was a woman. Her posture had always been bad, because of her embarrassment. Now she had a posture like a question mark.

She coughed. She laughed. She made a couple of jokes which I don't remember now.

Then she sent us away. "Don't look back," she said. So we didn't.

She died at about the same time of day that Uncle Alex died—an hour or two after the sun went down.

And hers would have been an unremarkable death statistically, if it were not for one detail, which was this: Her healthy husband, James Carmalt Adams, the editor of a trade journal for purchasing agents, which he put together in a cubicle on Wall Street, had died two mornings before—on "The Brokers' Special," the only train in American railroading history to hurl itself off an open drawbridge.

Think of that.

◆◆◆

This really happened.

◆◆◆

Bernard and I did not tell Alice about what had happened to her husband, who was supposed to take full charge of the children after she died, but she found out about it anyway. An ambulatory female patient gave her a copy of the New York *Daily News*. The front page headline was about the dive of the train. Yes, and there was a list of the dead and missing inside.

Since Alice had never received any religious instruction, and since she had led a blameless life, she never thought of her awful luck as being anything but accidents in a very busy place.

Good for her.

◆◆◆

Exhaustion, yes, and deep money worries, too, made her say toward the end that she guessed that she wasn't really very good at life.

Then again: Neither were Laurel and Hardy.

◆◆◆

My brother and I had already taken over her household. After she died, her three oldest sons, who were between the ages of eight and fourteen, held a meeting, which no grownups could attend. Then they came out and asked that we honor their only two requirements: That they remain together, and that they keep their two dogs. The youngest child, who was not at the meeting, was a baby only a year old or so.

From then on, the three oldest were raised by me and my wife, Jane Cox Vonnegut, along with our own three children, on Cape Cod. The baby, who lived with us for a while, was adopted by a first cousin of their father, who is now a judge in Birmingham, Alabama.

So be it.

The three oldest kept their dogs.

◆◆◆

I remember now what one of her sons, who is named "Kurt" like my father and me, asked me as we drove from New Jersey to Cape Cod with the two dogs in back. He was about eight.

We were going from south to north, so where we were going was "up" to him. There were just the two of us. His brothers had gone ahead.

"Are the kids up there nice?" he said.

"Yes, they are," I replied.

He is an airline pilot now.

They are all something other than children now.

◆◆◆

One of them is a goat farmer on a mountaintop in Jamaica. He has made come true a dream of our sister's: To live far from the madness of cities, with animals for friends. He has no telephone or electricity.

He is desperately dependent on rainfall. He is a ruined man, if it does not rain.

◆◆◆

The two dogs have died of old age. I used to roll around with them on rugs for hours on end, until they were all pooped out.

◆◆◆

Yes, and our sister's sons are candid now about a creepy business which used to worry them a lot: They cannot find their mother or their father in their memories anywhere—not anywhere.

The goat farmer, whose name is James Carmalt Adams, Jr., said this about it to me, tapping his forehead with his fingertips: "It isn't the museum it should be."

The museums in children's minds, I think, automatically empty themselves in times of utmost horror—to protect the children from eternal grief.

◆◆◆

For my own part, though: It would have been catastrophic if I had forgotten my sister at once. I had never told her so, but she was the person I had always written for. She was the secret of whatever artistic unity I had ever achieved. She was the secret of my technique. Any creation which has any wholeness and harmoniousness, I suspect, was made by an artist or inventor with an audience of one in mind.

Yes, and she was nice enough, or Nature was nice enough, to allow me to feel her presence for a number of years after she died—to let me go on writing for her. But then she began to fade away, perhaps because she had more important business elsewhere.

Be that as it may, she had vanished entirely as my audience by the time Uncle Alex died.

So the seat between my brother and me on the airplane seemed especially vacant to me. I filled it as best I could—with that morning's issue of *The New York Times*.

❖❖❖

While my brother and I waited for the plane to take off for Indianapolis, he made me a present of a joke by Mark Twain—about an opera Twain had seen in Italy. Twain said that he hadn't heard anything like it ". . . since the orphanage burned down."

We laughed.

❖❖❖

He asked me politely how my work was going. I think he respects but is baffled by my work.

I said that I was sick of it, but that I had always been sick of it. I told him a remark which I had heard attributed to the writer Renata Adler, who hates writing, that a writer was a person who hated writing.

I told him, too, what my agent, Max Wilkinson, wrote to me after I complained again about what a disagreeable profession I had. This was it: "Dear Kurt —I never knew a blacksmith who was in love with his anvil."

We laughed again, but I think the joke was partly

lost on my brother. His life has been an unending honeymoon with his anvil.

◆◆◆

I told him that I had been going to operas recently, and that the set for the first act of *Tosca* had looked exactly like the interior of Union Station in Indianapolis to me. While the actual opera was going on, I said, I daydreamed about putting track numbers in the archways of the set, and passing out bells and whistles to the orchestra, and staging an opera about Indianapolis during the Age of the Iron Horse.

"People from our great-grandfathers' generation would mingle with our own, when we were young—" I said, "and all the generations in between. Arrivals and departures would be announced. Uncle Alex would leave for his job as a spy in Baltimore. You would come home from your freshman year at M.I.T.

"There would be shoals of relatives," I said, "watching the travelers come and go—and black men to carry the luggage and shine the shoes."

◆◆◆

"Every so often in my opera," I said, "the stage would turn mud-colored with uniforms. That would be a war.

"And then it would clear up again."

◆◆◆

After the plane took off, my brother showed me a piece of scientific apparatus which he had brought along. It was a photoelectric cell connected to a small tape recorder. He aimed the electric eye at clouds. It perceived lightning flashes which were invisible to us in the dazzle of daytime.

The secret flashes were recorded as clicks by the recorder. We could also hear the clicks as they happened—on a tiny earphone.

"There's a hot one," my brother announced. He indicated a distant cumulus cloud, a seeming Pike's Peak of whipped cream.

He let me listen to the clicks. There were two quick ones, then some silence, then three quick ones, then silence again.

"How far away is that cloud?" I asked him.

"Oh—a hundred miles, maybe," he said.

I thought it was beautiful that my big brother could detect secrets so simply from so far away.

◆◆◆

I lit a cigarette.

Bernard doesn't smoke any more, because it is so important that he live a good while longer. He still has two little boys to raise.

◆◆◆

Yes, and while my big brother meditated about clouds, the mind I was given daydreamed the story in this book. It is about desolated cities and spiritual cannibalism and incest and loneliness and lovelessness and death, and so on. It depicts myself and my beautiful sister as monsters, and so on.

This is only natural, since I dreamed it on the way to a funeral.

◆◆◆

It is about this terribly old man in the ruins of Manhattan, you see, where almost everyone has been killed by a mysterious disease called "The Green Death."

He lives there with his illiterate, rickety, pregnant little granddaughter, Melody. Who is he really? I guess he is myself—experimenting with being old.

Who is Melody? I thought for a while that she was all that remained of my memory of my sister. I now believe that she is what I feel to be, when I experiment with old age, all that is left of my optimistic imagination, of my creativeness.

Hi ho.

◆◆◆

The old man is writing his autobiography. He begins it with words which my late Uncle Alex told me one time should be used by religious skeptics as a prelude to their nightly prayers.

These are the words: "To whom it may concern."

◆◆◆

Chapter 1

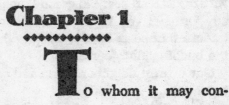

To whom it may concern:

It is springtime. It is late afternoon.

Smoke from a cooking fire on the terrazzo floor of the lobby of the Empire State Building on the Island of Death floats out over the ailanthus jungle which Thirty-fourth Street has become.

The pavement on the floor of the jungle is all crinkum-crankum—heaved this way and that by frostheaves and roots.

There is a small clearing in the jungle. A blue-eyed, lantern-jawed old white man, who is two meters tall and one hundred years old, sits in the clearing on what was once the back seat of a taxicab.

21

I am that man.

My name is Dr. Wilbur Daffodil-11 Swain.

◆◆◆

I am barefoot. I wear a purple toga made from draperies found in the ruins of the Americana Hotel.

I am a former President of the United States of America. I was the final President, the tallest President, and the only one ever to have been divorced while occupying the White House.

I inhabit the first floor of the Empire State Building with my sixteen-year-old granddaughter, who is Melody Oriole-2 von Peterswald, and with her lover, Isadore Raspberry-19 Cohen. The three of us have the building all to ourselves.

Our nearest neighbor is one and one-half kilometers away.

I have just heard one of her roosters crow.

◆◆◆

Our nearest neighbor is Vera Chipmunk-5 Zappa, a woman who loves life and is better at it than anyone I ever knew. She is a strong and warm-hearted and hard-working farmer in her early sixties. She is built like a fireplug. She has slaves whom she treats very well. And she and the slaves raise cattle and pigs and chickens and goats and corn and wheat and vegetables and fruits and grapes along the shores of the East River.

They have built a windmill for grinding grain, and

a still for making brandy, and a smokehouse—and on and on.

"Vera—" I told her the other day, "if you would only write us a new Declaration of Independence, you would be the Thomas Jefferson of modern times."

❖❖❖

I write this book on the stationery of the Continental Driving School, three boxes of which Melody and Isadore found in a closet on the sixty-fourth floor of our home. They also found a gross of ball-point pens.

❖❖❖

Visitors from the mainland are rare. The bridges are down. The tunnels are crushed. And boats will not come near us, for fear of the plague peculiar to this island, which is called "The Green Death."

And it is that plague which has earned Manhattan the sobriquet, "The Island of Death."

Hi ho.

❖❖❖

It is a thing I often say these days: "Hi ho." It is a kind of senile hiccup. I have lived too long.

Hi ho.

❖❖❖

The gravity is very light today. I have an erection as a result of that. All males have erections on days like this. They are automatic consequences of near-weightlessness. They have little to do with eroticism in most cases, and nothing to do with it in the life of a man my age. They are hydraulic experiences—the results of confused plumbing, and little more.

Hi ho.

◆◆◆

The gravity is so light today, that I feel as though I might scamper to the top of the Empire State Building with a manhole cover, and fling it into New Jersey.

That would surely be an improvement on George Washington's sailing a silver dollar across the Rappahannock. And yet some people insist that there is no such thing as progress.

◆◆◆

I am sometimes called "The King of Candlesticks," because I own more than one thousand candlesticks.

But I am fonder of my middle name, which is "Daffodil-11." And I have written this poem about it, and about life itself, of course:

> "I was those seeds,
> "I am this meat,
> "This meat hates pain,
> "This meat must eat.
> "This meat must sleep,
> "This meat must dream,

"This meat must laugh,
"This meat must scream.
"But when, as meat,
"It's had its fill,
"Please plant it as
"A Daffodil."

♦♦♦

And who will read all this? God knows. Not Melody and Isadore, surely. Like all the other young people on the island, they can neither read nor write.

They have no curiosity about the human past, nor about what life may be like on the mainland.

As far as they are concerned, the most glorious accomplishment of the people who inhabited this island so teemingly was to die, so we could have it all to ourselves.

I asked them the other evening to name the three most important human beings in history. They protested that the question made no sense to them.

I insisted that they put their heads together anyway, and give me some sort of answer, which they did. They were very sulky about the exercise. It was painful to them.

They finally came up with an answer. Melody does most of the talking for them, and this is what she said in all seriousness: "You, and Jesus Christ, and Santa Claus."

Hi ho.

◆◆◆

When I do not ask them questions, they are as happy as clams.

◆◆◆

They hope to become slaves of Vera Chipmunk-5 Zappa some day. That is O.K. with me.

◆◆◆

Chapter 2

ND I really will try to stop writing "Hi ho" all the time.

Hi ho.

◆◆◆

I was born right here in New York City. I was not then a *Daffodil*. I was christened Wilbur *Rockefeller* Swain.

I was not alone, moreover. I had a dizygotic twin, a female. She was named Eliza Mellon Swain.

We were christened in a hospital rather than in a church, and we were not surrounded by relatives and our parents' friends. The thing was: Eliza and I were so ugly that our parents were ashamed.

27

We were monsters, and we were not expected to live very long. We had six fingers on each little hand, and six toes on each little footsie. We had supernumerary nipples as well—two of them apiece.

We were not mongolian idiots, although we had the coarse black hair typical of mongoloids. We were something new. We were *neanderthaloids*. We had the features of adult, fossil human beings even in infancy—massive brow-ridges, sloping foreheads, and steamshovel jaws.

◆◆◆

We were supposed to have no intelligence, and to die before we were fourteen.

But I am still alive and kicking, thank you. And Eliza would be, too, I'm certain, if she had not been killed at the age of fifty—in an avalanche on the outskirts of the Chinese colony on the planet Mars.

Hi ho.

◆◆◆

Our parents were two silly and pretty and very young people named Caleb Mellon Swain and Letitia Vanderbilt Swain, née Rockefeller. They were fabulously well-to-do, and descended from Americans who had all but wrecked the planet with a form of Idiot's Delight—obsessively turning money into power, and then power back into money again, and then money back into power again.

But Caleb and Letitia were harmless themselves.

Father was very good at backgammon and so-so at color photography, they say. Mother was active in the National Association for the Advancement of Colored People. Neither worked. Neither was a college graduate, though both had tried.

They wrote and spoke nicely. They adored each other. They were humble about having done so poorly in schools. They were kind.

And I cannot fault them for being shattered by having given birth to monsters. Anyone would have been shattered by giving birth to Eliza and me.

◆◆◆

And Caleb and Letitia were at least as good at parenting as I was, when my turn rolled around. I was wholly indifferent to my own children, although they were normal in every way.

Perhaps I would have been more entertained by my children if they had been monsters like Eliza and me.

Hi ho.

◆◆◆

Young Caleb and Letitia were advised not to break their hearts and risk their furniture by attempting to raise Eliza and me in Turtle Bay. We were no more true relatives of theirs, their advisors said, than baby crocodiles.

Caleb's and Letitia's response was humane. It was also expensive and Gothic in the extreme. Our parents did not hide us in a private hospital for cases such as ours. They entombed us instead in a spooky old mansion which they had inherited—in the midst of two hundred acres of apple trees on a mountain-top, near the hamlet of Galen, Vermont.

No one had lived there for thirty years.

◆◆◆

Carpenters and electricians and plumbers were brought in to turn it into a sort of paradise for Eliza and me. Thick rubber padding was put under all the wall-to-wall carpets, so we would not hurt ourselves in case we fell. Our diningroom was lined with tile, and there were drains in the floor, so we and the room could be hosed off after every meal.

More important, perhaps, were two chain-link fences which went up. They were topped with barbed wire. The first enclosed the orchard. The second separated the mansion from the prying eyes of the workmen who had to be let in through the first from time to time in order to look after the apple trees.

Hi ho.

◆◆◆

A staff was recruited from the neighborhood. There was a cook. There were two cleaning women and a cleaning man. There were two practical nurses who fed us and dressed us and undressed us and bathed us. The one I remember best is Withers Witherspoon, a combination guard, chauffeur and handy-man.

His mother was a Withers. His father was a Wither-spoon.

◆◆◆

Yes, and these were simple country people, who, with the exception of Withers Witherspoon, who had been a soldier, had never been outside Vermont. They had rarely ventured more than ten miles from Galen, for that matter—and they were necessarily all related to one another, as inbred as Eskimos.

They were of course distantly related to Eliza and me, too, since our Vermont ancestors had once been content to dogpaddle endlessly, so to speak, in the same tiny genetic pool.

But, in the American scheme of things at that time, they were related to our family as carp were related to eagles, say—for our family had evolved into world-travelers and multimillionaires.

Hi ho.

◆◆◆

Yes, and it was easy for our parents to buy the fealty of these living fossils from the family past. They were given modest salaries which seemed enormous to them, since the money-making lobes of their brains were so primitive.

They were given pleasant apartments in the man-sion, and color television sets. They were encouraged to eat like emperors, charging whatever they liked to our parents. They had very little work to do.

Better still, they did not have to think much for themselves. They were placed under the command of a young general practitioner who lived in the hamlet, Dr. Stewart Rawlings Mott, who would look in on us every day.

Dr. Mott was a Texan, incidentally, a melancholy and private young man. To this day, I do not know what induced him to move so far from his people and his birthplace—to practice medicine in an Eskimo settlement in Vermont.

As a curious footnote in history, and a probably meaningless one: The grandson of Dr. Mott would become the King of Michigan during my second term as President of the United States.

I must hiccup again: Hi ho.

◆◆◆

I swear: If I live to complete this autobiography, I will go through it again, and cross out all the "Hi ho's."

Hi ho.

◆◆◆

Yes, and there was an automatic sprinkler system in the mansion—and burglar alarms on the windows and doors and skylights.

When we grew older and uglier, and capable of breaking arms or tearing heads off, a great gong was installed in the kitchen. This was connected to cherry red push-buttons in every room and at regular intervals down every corridor. The buttons glowed in the dark.

A button was to be pushed only if Eliza or I began to toy with murder.

Hi ho.

◆◆◆

Chapter 3

FATHER went to Galen with a lawyer and a physician and an architect—to oversee the refurbishing of the mansion for Eliza and me, and the hiring of the servants and Dr. Mott. Mother remained here in Manhattan, in their townhouse in Turtle Bay.

Turtles in great profusion, incidentally, have returned to Turtle Bay.

Vera Chipmunk-5 Zappa's slaves like to catch them for soup.

Hi ho.

◆◆◆

It was one of the few occasions, except for Father's death, when Mother and Father were separated for more than a day or two. And Father wrote a graceful letter to Mother from Vermont, which I found in Mother's bedside table after Mother died.

It may have been the whole of their correspondence by mail.

"My dearest Tish—" he wrote, "Our children will be very happy here. We can be proud. Our architect can be proud. The workmen can be proud.

"However short our children's lives may be, we will have given them the gifts of dignity and happiness. We have created a delightful asteroid for them, a little world with only one mansion on it, and otherwise covered with apple trees."

◆◆◆

Then he returned to an asteroid of his own—in Turtle Bay. He and Mother, thereafter, again on the advice of physicians, would visit us once a year, and always on our birthday.

Their brownstone still stands, and it is still snug and weathertight. It is there that our nearest neighbor, Vera Chipmunk-5 Zappa, now quarters her slaves.

◆◆◆

"And when Eliza and Wilbur die and go to Heaven at last," our father's letter went on, "we can lay them to rest among their Swain ancestors, in the private family cemetery out under the apple trees."

Hi ho.

◆◆◆

As for who was already buried in that cemetery, which was separated from the mansion by a fence: They were mostly Vermont apple farmers and their mates and offspring, people of no distinction. Many of them were no doubt nearly as illiterate and ignorant as Melody and Isadore.

That is to say: They were innocent great apes, with limited means for doing mischief, which, in my opinion as an old, old man, is all that human beings were ever meant to be.

◆◆◆

Many of the tombstones in the cemetery had sunk out of sight or capsized. Weather had dimmed the epitaphs of those which still stood.

But there was one tremendous monument, with thick granite walls, a slate roof, and great doors, which would clearly last past Judgment Day. It was the mausoleum of the founder of the family's fortune and the builder of our mansion, Professor Elihu Roosevelt Swain.

◆◆◆

Professor Swain was by far the most intelligent of all our known ancestors, I would say—Rockefellers, Du Ponts, Mellons, Vanderbilts, Dodges and all. He took a degree from the Massachusetts Institute of Technology at the age of eighteen, and went on to set up the Department of Civil Engineering at Cornell University at the age of twenty-two. By that time, he already had several important patents on railroad bridges and safety devices, which alone would soon have made him a millionaire.

But he was not content. So he created the Swain Bridge Company, which designed and supervised the construction of half the railroad bridges in the entire planet.

◆◆◆

He was a citizen of the world. He spoke many languages, and was the personal friend of many heads of state. But when it came time to build a palace of his own, he placed it among his ignorant ancestors' apple trees.

And he was the only person who loved that barbarous pile until Eliza and I came along. We were so happy there!

◆◆◆

And Eliza and I shared a secret with Professor Swain, even though he had been dead for half a century. The servants did not know it. Our parents did not know it. And the workmen who refurbished the place never suspected it, apparently, although they must have punched pipes and wires and heating ducts through all sorts of puzzling spaces.

This was the secret: There was a mansion concealed within the mansion. It could be entered

through trap doors and sliding panels. It consisted of
secret staircases and listening posts with peepholes,
and secret passageways. There were tunnels, too.

It was actually possible for Eliza and me, for example, to vanish into a huge grandfather clock in the
ballroom at the top of the northernmost tower, and
to emerge almost a kilometer away—through a trap
door in the floor of the mausoleum of Professor Elihu
Roosevelt Swain.

◆◆◆

We shared another secret with the Professor, too—
which we learned from going through some of his
papers in the mansion. His middle name hadn't actually been *Roosevelt*. He had given himself that middle name in order to seem more aristocratic when he
enrolled as a student at M.I.T.

His name on his baptismal certificate was Elihu
Witherspoon Swain.

It was from his example, I suppose, that Eliza and
I got the idea, eventually, of giving simply everybody
new middle names.

◆◆◆

Chapter 4

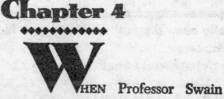

WHEN Professor Swain died, he was so fat that I do not see how he could have fitted into any of his secret passageways. They were very narrow. Eliza and I were able to fit into them, however, even when we were two meters tall —because the ceilings were so high—

Yes, and Professor Swain died of his fatness in the mansion, at a dinner he gave in honor of Samuel Langhorne Clemens and Thomas Alva Edison.

Those were the days.

Eliza and I found the menu. It began with turtle soup.

◆◆◆

Our servants would tell each other now and then that the mansion was haunted. They heard sneezing and cackling in the walls, and the creaking of stairways where there were no stairways, and the opening and shutting of doors where there were no doors.

Hi ho.

◆◆◆

It would be exciting for me to cry out, as a crazed old centenarian in the ruins of Manhattan, that Eliza and I were subjected to acts of unspeakable cruelty in that spooky old house. But we may have in fact been the two happiest children that history has so far known.

That ecstasy would not end until our fifteenth year.

Think of that.

Yes, and when I became a pediatrician, practicing rural medicine in the mansion where I was raised, I often told myself about this childish patient or that one, remembering my own childhood: "This person has just arrived on this planet, knows nothing about it, has no standards by which to judge it. This person does not care what it becomes. It is eager to become absolutely anything it is supposed to be."

That surely describes the state of mind of Eliza and me, when we were very young. And all the information we received about the planet we were on indicated that idiots were lovely things to be.

So we cultivated idiocy.

We refused to speak coherently in public. "Buh," and, "Duh," we said. We drooled and rolled our eyes. We farted and laughed. We ate library paste.

Hi ho.

◆◆◆

Consider: We were at the center of the lives of those who cared for us. They could be heroically Christian in their own eyes only if Eliza and I remained helpless and vile. If we became openly wise and self-reliant, they would become our drab and inferior assistants. If we became capable of going out into the world, they might lose their apartments, their color televisions, their illusions of being sorts of doctors and nurses, and their high-paying jobs.

So, from the very first, and without quite knowing what they were doing, I am sure, they begged us a thousand times a day to go on being helpless and vile.

There was only one small advancement they wished us to make up the ladder of human achievements. They hoped with all their hearts that we would become toilet-trained.

Again: We were glad to comply.

◆◆◆

But we could secretly read and write English by the time we were four. We could read and write French, German, Italian, Latin and ancient Greek by the time we were seven, and do calculus, too.

There were thousands of books in the mansion. By the time we were ten, we had read them all by candlelight, at naptime or after bedtime—in secret passageways, or often in the mausoleum of Elihu Roosevelt Swain.

◆◆◆

But we continued to drool and babble and so on, whenever grownups were around. It was fun.

We did not itch to display our intelligence in public. We did not think of intelligence as being useful or attractive in any way. We thought of it as being simply one more example of our freakishness, like our extra nipples and fingers and toes.

And we may have been right at that. You know? Hi ho.

◆◆◆

Chapter 5

AND meanwhile the strange young Dr. Stewart Rawlings Mott weighed us and measured us, and peered into our orifices, and took samples of our urine—day after day after day.

"How is everybody today?" he would say.

We would tell him "Bluh" and "Duh," and so on. We called him "Flocka Butt."

And we ourselves did all we could to make each day exactly like the one before. Whenever "Flocka Butt" congratulated us on our healthy appetites and regular bowel movements, for example, I would invariably stick my thumbs in my ears and waggle my fingers, and Eliza would hoist her skirt and snap the elastic at the waist of her pantyhose.

Eliza and I believed then what I believe even now:
That life can be painless, provided that there is sufficient peacefulness for a dozen or so rituals to be
repeated simply endlessly.

Life, ideally, I think, should be like the Minuet or
the Virginia Reel or the Turkey Trot, something easily mastered in a dancing school.

◆◆◆

I teeter even now between thinking that Dr. Mott
loved Eliza and me, and knew how smart we were,
and wished to protect us from the cruelties of the
outside world, and thinking that he was comatose.

After Mother died, I discovered that the linen
chest at the foot of her bed was crammed with pack-
ets of Dr. Mott's bi-weekly reports on the health of
Eliza and me. He told of the ever-greater quantities
of food being consumed and then excreted. He
spoke, too, of our unflagging cheerfulness, and our
natural resistance to common diseases of childhood.

The sorts of things he reported, in fact, were the
sorts of things a carpenter's helper would have had
no trouble detecting—such as that, at the age of nine,
Eliza and I were over two meters tall.

No matter how large Eliza and I became, though,
one figure remained constant in his reports: Our
mental age was between two and three.

Hi ho.

◆◆◆

"Flocka Butt," along with my sister, of course, is one of the few people I am really hungry to see in the afterlife.

I am dying to ask him what he really thought of us as children—how much he suspected, how much he really knew.

◆◆◆

Eliza and I must have given him thousands of clues as to our intelligence. We weren't the cleverest of deceivers. We were only children, after all.

It seems probable to me that, when we babbled in his presence, we used words from some foreign language which he could recognize. He may have gone into the library of the mansion, which was of no interest to the servants, and found the books somehow disturbed.

He may have discovered the secret passageways himself, through some accident. He used to wander around the house a great deal after he was through with us, I know, explaining to the servants that his father was an architect. He may have actually gone into the secret passageways, and found books we were reading in there, and seen that the floors were spattered with candlewax.

Who knows?

◆◆◆

I would like to know, too, what his secret sorrow was. Eliza and I, when we were young, were so wrapped up in each other that we rarely noticed the emotional condition of anybody else. But we were surely impressed by Dr. Mott's sadness. So it must have been profound.

◆◆◆

I once asked his grandson, the King of Michigan, Stewart Oriole-2 Mott, if he had any idea why Dr. Mott had found life to be such a crushing affair. "Gravity hadn't yet turned mean," I said. "The sky had not yet turned from blue to yellow, never to be blue again. The planet's natural resources had yet to come to an end. The country had not yet been depopulated by Albanian flu and The Green Death.

"Your grandfather had a nice little car and a nice little house and a nice little practice and a nice little wife and a nice little child," I said to the King. "And yet he used to *mope* so!"

My interview with the King took place, incidentally, in his palace on Lake Maxinkuckee, in northern Indiana, where Culver Military Academy had once stood. I was still nominally the President of the United States of America, but I had lost control of everything. There wasn't any Congress any more, or any system of Federal Courts, or any Treasury or Army or any of that.

There were probably only eight hundred people left in all of Washington, D.C. I was down to one employee when I paid my respects to the King.

Hi ho.

◆◆◆

He asked me if I regarded him as an enemy, and I said, "Heavens, no, Your Highness—I am delighted that someone of your calibre has brought law and order to the Middle West."

◆◆◆

He grew impatient with me when I pressed him to tell me more about his grandfather, Dr. Mott.

"Christ," he said, "what American knows anything about his grandparents?"

◆◆◆

He was a skinny and supple and ascetic young soldier-saint in those days. My granddaughter, Melody, would come to know him when he was an obscene voluptuary, a fat old man in robes encrusted with precious stones.

◆◆◆

He was wearing a simple soldier's tunic without any badges of rank when I met him.

As for my own costume: It was appropriately clownish—a top hat, a claw-hammer coat and striped pants, a pearl-gray vest with matching spats, a soiled white shirt with a choke collar and tie. The belly of my vest was festooned with a gold watch-chain which had belonged to John D. Rockefeller, the ancestor of mine who had founded Standard Oil.

Dangling from the watch-chain were my Phi Beta Kappa key from Harvard and a miniature plastic daffodil. My middle name had by then been legally changed from *Rockefeller* to *Daffodil-11*.

"There were no murders or embezzlements or suicides or drinking problems or drug problems in Dr. Mott's branch of the family," the King went on, "as far as I know."

He was thirty. I was seventy-nine.

"Maybe Grandfather was just one of those people who was *born* unhappy," he said. "Did you ever think of that?"

❖❖❖

Chapter 6

✦✦✦✦✦✦✦✦✦✦

PERHAPS some people really are born unhappy. I surely hope not.

Speaking for my sister and myself: We were born with the capacity and the determination to be utterly happy all the time.

Perhaps even in this we were freaks.

Hi ho.

✦✦✦

What is happiness?

In Eliza's and my case, happiness was being perpetually in each other's company, having plenty of servants and good food, living in a peaceful, book-filled mansion on an asteroid covered with apple trees, and growing up as specialized halves of a single brain.

Although we pawed and embraced each other a great deal, our intentions were purely intellectual. True—Eliza matured sexually at the age of seven. I, however, would not enter puberty until my last year in Harvard Medical School, at the age of twenty-three. Eliza and I used bodily contact only in order to increase the intimacy of our brains.

Thus did we give birth to a single genius, which died as quickly as we were parted, which was reborn the moment we got together again.

♦♦♦

We became almost cripplingly specialized as halves of that genius, which was the most important individual in our lives, but which we never named.

When we learned to read and write, for example, it was I who actually did the reading and writing. Eliza remained illiterate until the day she died.

But it was Eliza who did the great intuitive leaping for us both. It was Eliza who guessed that it would be in our best interests to remain speechless, but to become toilet-trained. It was Eliza who guessed what books were, and what the little marks on the pages might mean.

It was Eliza who sensed that there was something cockeyed about the dimensions of some of the mansion's rooms and corridors. And it was I who did the methodical work of taking actual measurements, and then probing the paneling and parquetry with screwdrivers and kitchen knives, seeking doors to an alternate universe, which we found.

Hi ho.

◆◆◆

Yes, I did all the reading. And it seems to me now that there is not a single book published in an Indo-European language before the First World War that I have not read aloud.

But it was Eliza who did the memorizing, and who told me what we had to learn next. And it was Eliza who could put seemingly unrelated ideas together in order to get a new one. It was Eliza who *juxtaposed.*

◆◆◆

Much of our information was hopelessly out of date, of course, since few new books had been brought into the mansion since 1912. Much of it, too, was timeless. And much of it was downright silly, such as the dances we learned to do.

If I wished, I could do a very presentable and historically accurate version of the Tarantella, here in the ruins of New York.

◆◆◆

Were Eliza and I really a genius, when we thought as one?

I have to say yes, especially in view of the fact that

we had no instructors. And I am not boasting when I say so, for I am only half of that fine mind.

We criticized Darwin's Theory of Evolution, I remember, on the grounds the creatures would become terribly vulnerable while attempting to improve themselves, while developing wings or armorplate, say. They would be eaten up by more practical animals, before their wonderful new features could be refined.

We made at least one prediction that was so deadly accurate that thinking about it even now leaves me thunderstruck.

Listen: We began with the mystery of how ancient peoples had erected the pyramids of Egypt and Mexico, and the great heads of Easter Island, and the barbaric arches of Stonehenge, without modern power sources and tools.

We concluded there must have been days of light gravity in olden times, when people could play tiddledy winks with huge chunks of stone.

We supposed that it might even be abnormal on earth for gravity to be stable for long periods of time. We predicted that at any moment gravity might become as capricious as winds and heat and cold, as blizzards and rainstorms again.

❖❖❖

Yes, and Eliza and I composed a precocious critique of the Constitution of the United States of America, too. We argued that it was as good a scheme for misery as any, since its success in keeping the common people reasonably happy and proud depended on the strength of the people themselves—and yet it described no practical machinery which would tend to make the people, as opposed to their elected representatives, strong.

We said it was possible that the framers of the Constitution were blind to the beauty of persons who were without great wealth or powerful friends or public office, but who were nonetheless genuinely strong.

We thought it was more likely, though, that the framers had not noticed that it was natural, and therefore almost inevitable, that human beings in extraordinary and enduring situations should think of themselves as composing new families. Eliza and I pointed out that this happened no less in democracies than in tyrannies, since human beings were the same the wide world over, and civilized only yesterday.

Elected representatives, hence, could be expected to become members of the famous and powerful family of elected representatives—which would, perfectly naturally, make them wary and squeamish and stingy with respect to all the other sorts of families which, again, perfectly naturally, subdivided mankind.

Eliza and I, thinking as halves of a single genius, proposed that the Constitution be amended so as to guarantee that every citizen, no matter how humble or crazy or incompetent or deformed, somehow be given membership in some family as covertly xenophobic and crafty as the one their public servants formed.

Good for Eliza and me!

◆◆◆

Hi ho.

◆◆◆

Chapter 7

◆◆◆◆◆◆◆◆◆◆

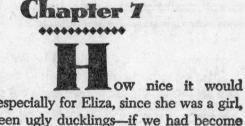ow nice it would have been, especially for Eliza, since she was a girl, if we had been ugly ducklings—if we had become beautiful by and by. But we simply grew more preposterous with each passing day.

There were a few advantages to being a male 2 meters tall. I was respected as a basketball player at prep school and college, even though I had very narrow shoulders and a voice like a piccolo, and not the first hints of a beard or pubic hair. Yes, and later on, after my voice had deepened and I ran as a candidate for Senator from Vermont, I was able to say on my billboards, "It takes a Big Man to do a Big Job!"

But Eliza, who was exactly as tall as I was, could not expect to be welcomed anywhere. There was no conceivable conventional role for a female which could be bent so as to accommodate a twelve-fingered, twelve-toed, four-breasted, Neanderthaloid half-genius—weighing one quintal, and two meters tall.

◆◆◆

Even as little children we knew we weren't ever going to win any beauty contests.

Eliza said something prophetic about that, incidentally. She couldn't have been more than eight. She said that maybe she could win a beauty contest on Mars.

She was, of course, destined to *die* on Mars.

Eliza's beauty prize there would be an avalanche of iron pyrite, better known as "Fool's Gold."

Hi ho.

◆◆◆

There was a time in our childhood when we actually agreed that we were *lucky* not to be beautiful. We knew from all the romantic novels I'd read out loud in my squeaky voice, often with gestures, that beautiful people had their privacy destroyed by passionate strangers.

We didn't want that to happen to us, since the two of us alone composed not only a single mind but a thoroughly populated Universe.

56

◆◆◆

This much I must say about our appearance, at least: Our clothing was the finest that money could buy. Our astonishing dimensions, which changed radically almost from month to month, were mailed off regularly, in accordance with our parents' instructions, to some of the finest tailors and cobblers and dressmakers and shirtmakers and haberdashers in the world.

The practical nurses who dressed and undressed us took a childish delight, even though we never went anywhere, in costuming us for imaginary social events for millionaires—for tea dances, for horse shows, for skiing vacations, for attending classes at expensive prep schools, for an evening of theater here in Manhattan and a supper afterwards with lots of champagne.

And so on.

Hi ho.

◆◆◆

We were aware of all the comedy in this. But, as brilliant as we were when we put our heads together, we did not guess until we were fifteen that we were also in the midst of a tragedy. We thought that ugliness was simply amusing to people in the outside world. We did not realize that we could actually nauseate strangers who came upon us unexpectedly.

We were so innocent as to the importance of good

looks, in fact, that we could see little point to the story of "The Ugly Duckling," which I read out loud to Eliza one day—in the mausoleum of Professor Elihu Roosevelt Swain.

The story, of course, was about a baby bird that was raised by ducks, who thought it was the funniest-looking duck they had ever seen. But then it turned out to be a swan when it grew up.

Eliza, I remember, said she thought it would have been a much better story if the little bird had waddled up on shore and turned into a rhinoceros.

Hi ho.

◆◆◆

Chapter 8

◆◆◆◆◆◆◆◆◆◆

UNTIL the eve of our fifteenth birthday, Eliza and I never heard anything bad about ourselves when we eavesdropped from the secret passageways.

The servants were so used to us that they hardly ever mentioned us, even in moments of deepest privacy. Dr. Mott seldom commented on anything but our appetites and our excretions. And our parents were so sickened by us that they were tongue-tied when they made their annual space voyage to our asteroid. Father, I remember, would talk to Mother rather haltingly and listlessly about world events he had read about in news magazines.

They would bring us toys from F.A.O. Schwarz—

guaranteed by that emporium to be educational for three-year-olds.

Hi ho.

◆◆◆

Yes, and I think now about all the secrets about the human condition I withhold from young Melody and Isadore, for their own peace of mind—the fact that the human afterlife is no good, and so on.

And then I am awed yet again by the perfect Lulu of a secret that was concealed from Eliza and me so long: That our own parents wished we would hurry up and die.

◆◆◆

We imagined lazily that our fifteenth birthday would be like all the rest. We put on the show we had always put on. Our parents arrived at our suppertime, which was four in the afternoon. We would get our presents the next day.

We threw food at each other in our tile-lined diningroom. I hit Eliza with an avocado. She hit me with a filet mignon. We bounced Parker House rolls off the maid. We pretended not to know that our parents had arrived and were watching us through a crack in the door.

Yes, and then, still not having greeted our parents face-to-face, we were bathed and talcumed, and dressed in our pajamas and bathrobes and bedroom slippers. Bedtime was at five, for Eliza and I pretended to sleep sixteen hours a day.

Our practical nurses, who were Oveta Cooper and Mary Selwyn Kirk, told us that there was a wonderful surprise waiting for us in the library.

We pretended to be gaga about what that surprise could possibly be.

We were full-grown giants by then.

I carried a rubber tugboat, which was supposedly my favorite toy. Eliza had a red velvet ribbon in the mare's nest of her coal black hair.

◆◆◆

As always, there was a large coffee table between Eliza and me and our parents when we were brought in. As always, our parents had brandy to sip. As always, there was a fizzing, popping blaze of pine and sappy apple logs in the fireplace. As always, an oil painting of Professor Elihu Roosevelt Swain over the mantelpiece beamed down on the ritual scene.

As always, our parents stood. They smiled up at us with what we still did not recognize as bittersweet dread.

As always, we pretended to find them adorable, but not to remember who they were at first.

◆◆◆

As always, Father did the talking.

"How do you do, Eliza and Wilbur?" he said. "You are looking very well. We are very glad to see you. Do you remember who we are?"

Eliza and I consulted with one another uneasily, drooling, and murmuring in ancient Greek. Eliza said to me in Greek, I remember, that she could not believe that we were related to such pretty dolls.

Father helped us out. He told us the name we had given to him years ago. "I am Bluth-luh," he said.

Eliza and I pretended to be flabbergasted. "Bluth-luh!" we told each other. We could not believe our good fortune. "Bluth-luh! Bluth-luh!" we cried.

"And this," said Father, indicating Mother, "is Mub-lub."

This was even more sensational news to Eliza and me. "Mub-lub! Mub-lub!" we exclaimed.

And now Eliza and I made a great intellectual leap, as always. Without any hints from anybody, we concluded that, if our parents were in the house, then our birthday must be close at hand. We chanted our idiot word for birthday, which was "Fuff-bay."

As always, we pretended to become overexcited. We jumped up and down. We were so big by then that the floor began to go up and down like a trampoline.

But we suddenly stopped, pretending, as always, to have been rendered catatonic by more happiness than was good for us.

That was always the end of the show. After that, we were led away.

Hi ho.

◆◆◆

Chapter 9

E were put into custom-made cribs—in separate but adjacent bedrooms. The rooms were connected by a secret panel in the wall. The cribs were as big as railroad flatcars. They made a terrible clatter when their sides were raised.

Eliza and I pretended to fall asleep at once. After a half an hour, however, we were reunited in Eliza's room. The servants never looked in on us. Our health was perfect, after all, and we had established a reputation for being, as they said, ". . . as good as gold at bedtime."

Yes, and we went through a trapdoor under Eliza's crib, and were soon taking turns watching our parents in the library—through a tiny hole we ourselves had drilled through the wall,.and through the upper corner of the frame around the painting of Professor Elihu Roosevelt Swain.

◆◆◆

Father was telling mother of a thing he had read in a news magazine on the day before. It seemed that scientists in the People's Republic of China were experimenting with making human beings smaller, so they would not need to eat so much and wear such big clothes.

Mother was staring into the fire. Father had to tell her twice about the Chinese rumor. The second time he did it, she replied emptily that she supposed that the Chinese could accomplish just about anything they put their minds to.

Only about a month before, the Chinese had sent two hundred explorers to Mars—without using a space vehicle of any kind.

No scientist in the Western World could guess how the trick was done. The Chinese themselves volunteered no details.

◆◆◆

Mother said that it seemed like such a long time since Americans had discovered anything. "All of a sudden," she said, "everything is being discovered by the Chinese."

◆◆◆

"We used to discover everything," she said.

◆◆◆

It was such a *stupefied* conversation. The level of animation was so low that our beautiful young parents from Manhattan might have been up to their necks in honey. They appeared, as they had always appeared to Eliza and me, to be under some curse which required them to speak only of matters which did not interest them at all.

And indeed they *were* under a malediction. But Eliza and I had not guessed its nature: That they were all but strangled and paralyzed by the wish that their own children would die.

And I promise this about our parents, although the only proof I have is a feeling in my bones: Neither one had ever suggested in any way to the other that he or she wished we would die.

Hi ho.

◆◆◆

But then there was a *bang* in the fireplace. Steam had to escape from a trap in a sappy log.

Yes, and Mother, because she was a symphony of chemical reactions like all other living things, gave a terrified shriek. Her chemicals insisted that she shriek in response to the *bang*.

After the chemicals got her to do that, though, they wanted a lot more from her. They thought it was high time she said what she really felt about Eliza and me, which she did. All sorts of other things went haywire when she said it. Her hands closed convulsively. Her spine buckled and her face shriveled to turn her into an old, old witch.

"I hate them, I hate them, I hate them," she said.

◆◆◆

And not many seconds passed before Mother said with spitting explicitness who it was she hated.

"I hate Wilbur Rockefeller Swain and Eliza Mellon Swain," she said.

◆◆◆

Chapter 10

✦✦✦✦✦✦✦✦✦✦

MOTHER was temporarily insane that night.

I got to know her well in later years. And, while I never learned to love her, or to love anyone, for that matter, I did admire her unwavering decency toward one and all. She was not a mistress of insults. When she spoke either in public or in private, no reputations died.

So it was not truly our mother who said on the eve of our fifteenth birthday, "How can I love Count Dracula and his blushing bride?"—meaning Eliza and me.

It was not truly our mother who asked our father, "How on Earth did I ever give birth to a pair of drooling totem poles?"

And so on.

◆◆◆

As for Father: He engulfed her in his arms. He was weeping with love and pity.

"Caleb, oh Caleb—" she said in his arms, "this isn't me."

"Of course not," he said.

"Forgive me," she said.

"Of course," he said.

"Will God ever forgive me?" she said.

"He already has," he said.

"It was as though a devil all of a sudden got inside of me," she said.

"That's what it was, Tish," he said.

Her madness was subsiding now. "Oh, Caleb—" she said.

◆◆◆

Lest I seem to be fishing for sympathy, let me say right now that Eliza and I in those days were about as emotionally vulnerable as the Great Stone Face in New Hampshire.

We needed a mother's and father's love about

as much as a fish needs a bicycle, as the saying goes.

So when our mother spoke badly of us, even wished we would die, our response was intellectual. We enjoyed solving problems. Perhaps Mother's problem was one we could solve—short of suicide, of course.

She pulled herself together again eventually. She steeled herself for another hundred birthdays with Eliza and me, in case God wished to test her in that way. But, before she did that, she said this:

"I would give anything, Caleb, for the faintest sign of intelligence, the merest flicker of humanness in the eyes of either twin."

◆◆◆

This was easily arranged.

Hi ho.

◆◆◆

So Eliza and I went back to Eliza's room, and we painted a big sign on a bedsheet. Then, after our parents were sound asleep, we stole into their room through the false back in an armoire. We hung the sign on the wall, so it would be the first thing they saw when they woke up.

This is what it said:

DEAR MATER AND PATER: WE CAN NEVER BE PRETTY
BUT WE CAN BE AS SMART OR AS DUMB AS THE WORLD
REALLY WANTS US TO BE.

> YOUR FAITHFUL SERVANTS,
> ELIZA MELLON SWAIN
> WILBUR ROCKEFELLER SWAIN

Hi ho.

◆◆◆

Chapter 11

◆◆◆◆◆◆◆◆◆◆

THUS did Eliza and I destroy our Paradise—our nation of two.

◆◆◆

We arose the next morning before our parents did, before the servants could come to dress us. We sensed no danger. We supposed ourselves still to be in Paradise as we dressed ourselves.

I chose to wear a conservative blue, pinstripe, three-piece suit, I remember. Eliza chose to wear a cashmere sweater, a tweed skirt, and pearls.

We agreed that Eliza should be our spokesman at first, since she had a rich alto voice. My voice did not have the authority to announce calmingly but convincingly that, in effect, the world had just turned upside down.

Remember, please, that almost all that anyone had ever heard us say up to then was "Buh" and "Duh," and so on.

Now we encountered Oveta Cooper, our practical nurse, in the colonnaded green marble foyer. She was startled to see us up and dressed.

Before she could comment on this, though, Eliza and I leaned our heads together, put them in actual contact, just above our ears. The single genius we composed thereby then spoke to Oveta in Eliza's voice, which was as lovely as a viola.

This is what that voice said:

"Good morning, Oveta. A new life begins for all of us today. As you can see and hear, Wilbur and I are no longer idiots. A miracle has taken place overnight. Our parents' dreams have come true. We are healed.

"As for you, Oveta: You will keep your apartment and your color television, and perhaps even receive a salary increase—as a reward for all you did to make this miracle come to pass. No one on the staff will experience any change, except for this one: Life here will become even easier and more pleasant than it was before."

Oveta, a bleak, Yankee dumpling, was hypnotized —like a rabbit who has met a rattlesnake. But Eliza and I were not a rattlesnake. With our heads together, we were one of the gentlest geniuses the world has ever known.

◆◆◆

"We will not be using the tiled diningroom any more," said Eliza's voice. "We have lovely manners, as you shall see. Please have our breakfast served in the solarium, and notify us when Mater and Pater are up and around. It would be very nice if, from now on, you would address my brother and me as 'Master Wilbur' and 'Mistress Eliza.'

"You may go now, and tell the others about the miracle."

Oveta remained transfixed. I at last had to snap my fingers under her nose to wake her up.

She curtseyed. "As you wish, Mistress Eliza," she said. And she went to spread the news.

◆◆◆

As we settled ourselves in the solarium, the rest of the staff straggled in humbly—to have a look at the young master and the young mistress we had become.

We greeted them by their full names. We asked them friendly questions which indicated that we had a detailed understanding of their lives. We apologized for having perhaps shocked some of them for changing so quickly.

"We simply did not realize," Eliza said, "that anybody *wanted* us to be intelligent."

We were by then so in charge of things that I, too, dared to speak of important matters. My high voice wouldn't be silly any more.

"With your cooperation," I said, "we will make this mansion famous for intelligence as it has been infamous for idiocy in days gone by. Let the fences come down."

"Are there any questions?" said Eliza.

There were none.

◆◆◆

Somebody called Dr. Mott.

◆◆◆

Our mother did not come down to breakfast. She remained in bed—petrified.

Father came down alone. He was wearing his nightclothes. He had not shaved. Young as he was, he was palsied and drawn.

Eliza and I were puzzled that he did not look happier. We hailed him not only in English, but in several other languages we knew.

It was to one of these foreign salutations that he responded at last. "Bon jour," he said.

"Sit thee doon! Sit thee doon!" said Eliza merrily.

The poor man sat.

◆◆◆

He was sick with guilt, of course, over having allowed intelligent human beings, his own flesh and blood, to be treated like idiots for so long.

Worse: His conscience and his advisors had told him before that it was all right if he could not love us, since we were incapable of deep feelings, and since there was nothing about us, objectively, that anyone in his right mind *could* love. But now it was his *duty* to love us, and he did not think he could do it.

He was horrified to discover what our mother knew she would discover, if she came downstairs: That intelligence and sensitivity in monstrous bodies like Eliza's and mine merely made us more repulsive.

This was not Father's fault or Mother's fault. It was not anybody's fault. It was as natural as breathing to all human beings, and to all warm-blooded creatures, for that matter, to wish quick deaths for monsters. This was an instinct.

And now Eliza and I had raised that instinct to intolerable tragedy.

Without knowing what we were doing, Eliza and I were putting the traditional curse of monsters on normal creatures. We were asking for respect.

❖❖❖

Chapter 12

✦✦✦✦✦✦✦✦✦

IN the midst of all the excitement, Eliza and I allowed our heads to be separated by several feet—so we were not thinking brilliantly any more.

We became dumb enough to think that Father was merely sleepy. So we made him drink coffee, and we tried to wake him up with some songs and riddles we knew.

I remember I asked him if he knew why cream was so much more expensive than milk.

He mumbled that he didn't know the answer.

So Eliza told him, "It's because the cows hate to squat on the little bottles."

We laughed about that. We rolled on the floor. And

then Eliza got up and stood over him, with her hands on her hips, and scolded him affectionately, as though he were a little boy. "Oh, what a sleepy-head!" she said. "Oh, what a sleepy-head!"

At that moment, Dr. Stewart Rawlings Mott arrived.

❖❖❖

Although Dr. Mott had been told on the telephone about Eliza's and my sudden metamorphosis, the day was like any other day to him, seemingly. He said what he always said when he arrived at the mansion: "And how is everybody today?"

I now spoke the first intelligent sentence Dr. Mott had ever heard from me. "Father won't wake up," I said.

"Won't he, now?" he replied. He rewarded the completeness of my sentence with the faintest of smiles.

Dr. Mott was so unbelievably bland, in fact, that he turned away from us to chat with Oveta Cooper, the practical nurse. Her mother had apparently been sick down in the hamlet. "Oveta—" he said, "you'll be pleased to know that your mother's temperature is almost normal."

Father was angered by this casualness, and no doubt glad to find someone with whom he could be openly angry.

"How long has this been going on, Doctor?" he wanted to know. "How long have you known about their intelligence?"

Dr. Mott looked at his watch. "Since about forty-two minutes ago," he said.

"You don't seem in the least surprised," said Father.

Dr. Mott appeared to think this over, then he shrugged. "I'm certainly very *happy* for everybody," he said.

I think it was the fact that Dr. Mott himself did not look at all happy when he said that which caused Eliza and me to put our heads together again. Something very queer was going on that we badly needed to understand.

◆◆◆

Our genius did not fail us. It allowed us to understand the truth of the situation—that we were somehow more tragic than ever.

But our genius, like all geniuses, suffered periodic fits of monumental naïveté. It did so now. It told us that all we had to do to make everything all right again was to return to idiocy.

"Buh," said Eliza.

"Duh," I said.

I farted.

Eliza drooled.

I picked up a buttered scone and threw it at the head of Oveta Cooper.

Eliza turned to Father. "Bluth-luh!" she said.

"Fuff-bay!" I cried.

Father cried.

◆◆◆

Chapter 13

◆◆◆◆◆◆◆◆◆◆◆

SIX days have passed since I began to write this memoir. On four of the days, the gravity was medium—what it used to be in olden times. It was so heavy yesterday, that I could hardly get out of bed, out of my nest of rags in the lobby of the Empire State Building. When I had to go to the elevator shaft we use for a toilet, making my way through the thicket of candlesticks I own, I crawled on all fours.

Hi ho.

Well—the gravity was light on the first day, and it is light again today. I have an erection again, and so does Isadore, the lover of my granddaughter Melody. So does every male on the island.

◆◆◆

Yes, and Melody and Isadore have packed a picnic lunch, and have gone bounding up to the intersection of Broadway and Forty-second Street, where, on days of light gravity, they are building a rustic pyramid.

They do not shape the slabs and chunks and boulders they put into it, and neither do they limit their materials to masonry. They throw in I-beams and oil drums and tires and automobile parts and office furniture and theater seats, too, and all manner of junk. But I have seen the results, and what they are building will not be an amorphous trash-pile when it is done. It will clearly be a pyramid.

◆◆◆

Yes, and if archaeologists of the future find this book of mine, they will be spared the fruitless labor of digging through the pyramid in search of its meaning. There are no secret treasure rooms in there, no chambers of any kind.

Its meaning, which is minuscule in any event, lies beneath the manhole cover over which the pyramid is constructed. It is the body of a stillborn male.

The infant is enclosed in an ornate box which was once a humidor for fine cigars. That box was placed on the floor of the manhole four years ago, amid all the cables and pipes down there—by Melody, who was its mother at the age of twelve, and by me, who was its great-grandfather, and by our nearest neighbor and dearest friend, Vera Chipmunk-5 Zappa.

The pyramid itself is entirely the idea of Melody and Isadore, who became her lover later on. It is a monument to a life that was never lived—to a person who was never named.

Hi ho.

◆◆◆

It is not necessary to dig through the pyramid to reach the box. It can be reached through other manholes.

Beware of rats.

◆◆◆

Since the infant was an heir of mine, the pyramid might be called this: "The Tomb of the Prince of Candlesticks."

◆◆◆

The name of the father of the Prince of Candlesticks is unknown. He forced his attentions on Melody on the outskirts of Schenectady. She was on her way from Detroit, in the Kingdom of Michigan, to the Island of Death, where she hoped to find her grandfather, who was the legendary Dr. Wilbur Daffodil-11 Swain.

◆◆◆

Melody is pregnant again—this time by Isadore.

She is a bow-legged little thing, rickety and snaggle-toothed, but cheerful. She ate very badly as a child—as an orphan in the harem of the King of Michigan.

Melody sometimes looks to me like a merry old Chinese woman, although she is only sixteen. A pregnant girl who looks like that is a sad thing for a pediatrician to see.

But the love that the robust and rosy Isadore gives her counterbalances my sadness with joy. Like almost all the members of his family, the Raspberries, Isadore has nearly all his teeth, and remains upright even when the gravity is most severe. He carries Melody around in his arms on days like that, and has offered to carry me.

The Raspberries are food-gatherers, mainly, living in and around the ruins of the New York Stock Exchange. They fish off docks. They mine for canned goods. They pick fruits and berries they find. They grow their own tomatoes and potatoes, and radishes, and little more.

They trap rats and bats and dogs and cats and birds, and eat them. A Raspberry will eat anything.

❖❖❖

Chapter 14

◆◆◆◆◆◆◆◆◆◆

I wish Melody what our parents once wished Eliza and me: A short but happy life on an asteroid.

Hi ho.

◆◆◆

Yes, and I have already said, Eliza and I might have had a long and happy life on an asteroid, if we had not showed off our intelligence one day. We might have been in the mansion still, burning the trees and the furniture and the bannisters and the paneling for warmth, and drooling and babbling when strangers came.

We could have raised chickens. We could have had a little vegetable garden. And we could have amused ourselves with our ever-increasing wisdom, caring nothing for its possible usefulness.

◆◆◆

The sun is going down. Thin clouds of bats stream out from the subway—jittering, squeaking, dispersing like gas. As always, I shudder.

I can't think of their noise as a noise. It is a disease of silence instead.

◆◆◆

I write on—in the light of a burning rag in a bowl of animal fat.

I have a thousand candlesticks, but no candles.

Melody and Isadore play backgammon—on a board I painted on the lobby floor.

They double and redouble each other, and laugh.

◆◆◆

They are planning a party for my one hundred and first birthday, which is a month away.

I eavesdrop on them sometimes. Old habits are hard to break. Vera Chipmunk-5 Zappa is making new costumes for the occasion—for herself and her slaves. She has mountains of cloth in her storerooms in Turtle Bay. The slaves will wear pink pantaloons and golden slippers, and green silk turbans with ostrich feather plumes, I heard Melody say.

Vera will be borne to the party in a sedan chair, I've heard, surrounded by slaves carrying presents and food and drink and torches, and frightening away wild dogs with the clangor of dinnerbells.

Hi ho.

❖❖❖

I must be very careful with my drinking at my birthday party. If I drank too much, I might spill the beans to everybody: That the life that awaits us after death is infinitely more tiresome than this one.

Hi ho.

❖❖❖

Chapter 15

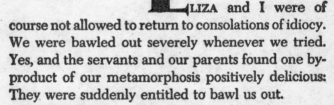

ELIZA and I were of course not allowed to return to consolations of idiocy. We were bawled out severely whenever we tried. Yes, and the servants and our parents found one by-product of our metamorphosis positively delicious: They were suddenly entitled to bawl us out.

What hell we caught from time to time!

◆◆◆

Yes, and Dr. Mott was fired, and all sorts of experts were brought in.

It was fun for a while. The first doctors to arrive were specialists in hearts and lungs and kidneys and so on. When they studied us organ by organ and body fluid by body fluid, we were masterpieces of health.

They were genial. They were all family employees in a way. They were research people whose work was financed by the Swain Foundation in New York. That was how they had been so easily rounded up and brought to Galen. The family had helped them. Now they would help the family.

They joshed us a lot. One of them, I remember, said to me that it must be fun to be so tall. "What's the weather up there like?" he said, and so on.

The joshing had a soothing effect. It gave us the mistaken impression that it did not matter how ugly we were. I still remember what an ear, nose and throat specialist said when he looked up into Eliza's enormous sinus cavities with a flashlight. "My God, nurse—" he said, "call up the National Geographic Society. We have just discovered a new entrance to Mammoth Cave!"

Eliza laughed. The nurse laughed. I laughed. We all laughed.

Our parents were in another part of the mansion. They kept away from all the fun.

◆◆◆

That early in the game, though, we had our first disturbing tastes of separation. Some of the examinations required that we be several rooms apart. As the distance between Eliza and me increased, I felt as though my head were turning to wood.

I became stupid and insecure.

When I was reunited with Eliza, she said that she had felt very much the same sort of thing. "It was as though my skull was filling up with maple syrup," she said.

And we bravely tried to be amused rather than

frightened by the listless children we became when we were parted. We pretended they had nothing to do with us, and we made up names for them. We called them "Betty and Bobby Brown."

◆◆◆

And now is as good a time as any, I think, to say that when we read Eliza's will, after her death in a Martian avalanche, we learned that she wished to be buried wherever she died. Her grave was to be marked with a simple stone, engraved with this information and nothing more:

HERE
LIES
BETTY
BROWN

◆◆◆

Yes, and it was the last specialist to look us over, a psychologist, Dr. Cordelia Swain Cordiner, who decreed that Eliza and I should be separated permanently, should, so to speak, become forever Betty and Bobby Brown.

◆◆◆

Chapter 16

ＦĒDOR Mikhailovich Dostoevski, the Russian novelist, said one time that, "One sacred memory from childhood is perhaps the best education." I can think of another quickie education for a child, which, in its way, is almost as salutary: Meeting a human being who is tremendously respected by the adult world, and realizing that that person is actually a malicious lunatic.

That was Eliza's and my experience with Dr. Cordelia Swain Cordiner, who was widely believed to be the greatest expert on psychological testing in the world—with the possible exception of China. Nobody knew what was going on in China any more.

◆◆◆

I have an Encyclopaedia Britannica here in the lobby
of the Empire State Building, which is the reason I
am able to give Dostoevski his middle name.

◆◆◆

Dr. Cordelia Swain Cordiner was invariably impres-
sive and gracious when in the presence of grownups.
She was elaborately dressed the whole time she was
in the mansion—in high-heeled shoes and fancy
dresses and jewelry.

We heard her tell our parents one time: "Just because a woman has three doctors' degrees and heads
a testing corporation which bills three million dollars
a year, that doesn't mean she can't be feminine."

When she got Eliza and me alone, though, she
seethed with paranoia.

"None of your tricks, no more of your snotty little
kid millionaire tricks with me," she would say.

And Eliza and I hadn't done *anything* wrong.

◆◆◆

She was so enraged by how much money and power
our family had, and so sick, that I don't think she
even noticed how huge and ugly Eliza and I were.
We were just two more rotten-spoiled little rich kids
to her.

"I wasn't born with any silver spoon in my mouth,"
she told us, not once but many times. "Many was the

day we didn't know where the next meal was coming from," she said. "Have you any idea what that's like?"

"No," said Eliza.

"Of course not," said Dr. Cordiner.

And so on.

◆◆◆

Since she was paranoid, it was especially unfortunate that her middle name was the same as our last name.

"I'm not your sweet Aunt Cordelia," she would say. "You needn't worry your little aristocratic brains about that. When my grandfather came from Poland, he changed his name from Stankowitz to Swain." Her eyes were blazing. "Say 'Stankowitzl' "

We said it.

"Now say 'Swain,' " she said.

We did.

◆◆◆

And finally one of us asked her what she was so mad about.

This made her very calm. "I am not mad," she said. "It would be very unprofessional for me to ever get mad about anything. However, let me say that asking a person of my calibre to come all this distance into the wilderness to personally administer tests to only two children is like asking Mozart to tune a piano. It is like asking Albert Einstein to balance a checkbook. Am I getting through to you, 'Mistress Eliza and Master Wilbur,' as I believe you are called?"

"Then why did you come?" I asked her.

Her rage came out into the open again. She said this to me with all possible nastiness: "Because money talks, 'Little Lord Fauntleroy.'"

◆◆◆

We were further shocked when we learned that she meant to administer tests to us separately. We said innocently that we would get many more correct answers if we were allowed to put our heads together.

She became a tower of irony. "Why, of course, Master and Mistress," she said. "And wouldn't you like to have an encyclopaedia in the room with you, too, and maybe the faculty of Harvard University, to tell you the answers, in case you're not sure?"

"That would be *nice*," we said.

"In case nobody has told you," she said, "this is the United States of America, where nobody has a right to rely on anybody else—where everybody learns to make his or her own way.

"I'm here to test you," she said, "but there's a basic rule for life I'd like to teach you, too, and you'll thank me for it in years to come."

This was the lesson: "Paddle your own canoe," she said. "Can you say that and remember it?"

Not only could I say it, but I remember it to this day: "Paddle your own canoe."

Hi ho.

◆◆◆

So we paddled our own canoes. We were tested as individuals at the stainless steel table in the tile-lined diningroom. When one of us was in there with Dr. Cordiner, with "Aunt Cordelia," as we came to call her in private, the other one was taken as far away as possible—to the ballroom at the top of the tower at the north end of the mansion.

Withers Witherspoon had the job of watching whichever one of us was in the ballroom. He was chosen for the job because he had been a soldier at one time. We heard "Aunt Cordelia's" instructions to him. She asked him to be alert to clues that Eliza and I were communicating telepathically.

Western science, with a few clues from the Chinese, had at last acknowledged that some people could communicate with certain others without visible or audible signals. The transmitters and receivers for such spooky messages were on the surfaces of sinus cavities, and those cavities had to be healthy and clear of obstructions.

The chief clue which the Chinese gave the West was this puzzling sentence, delivered in English, which took years to decipher: "I feel so lonesome when I get hay fever or a cold."

Hi ho.

◆◆◆

Well, mental telepathy was useless to Eliza and me over distances greater than three meters. With one of us in the diningroom, and the other in the ballroom, our bodies might as well have been on different planets—which is in fact their condition today.

Oh, sure—and I could take written examinations, but Eliza could not. When "Aunt Cordelia" tested Eliza, she had to read each question out loud to her, and then write down her answer.

And it seemed to us that we missed absolutely every question. But we must have answered a few correctly, for Dr. Cordiner reported to our parents that our intelligence was ". . . low normal for their age."

She said further, not knowing that we were eavesdropping, that Eliza would probably never learn to read or write, and hence could never be a voter or hold a driver's license. She tried to soften this some by observing that Eliza was ". . . quite an amusing chatterbox."

She said that I was ". . . a good boy, a serious boy —easily distracted by his scatter-brained sister. He reads and writes, but has a poor comprehension of the meanings of words and sentences. If he were separated from his sister, there is every reason to believe that he could become a fillingstation attendant or a janitor in a village school. His prospects for a happy and useful life in a rural area are fair to good."

❖❖❖

The People's Republic of China was at that very moment secretly creating literally millions upon millions of geniuses—by teaching pairs or small groups of congenial, telepathically compatible specialists to think as single minds. And those patchwork minds were the equals of Sir Isaac Newton's or William Shakespeare's, say.

Oh, yes—and long before I became President of the United States of America, the Chinese had begun to combine those synthetic minds into intellects so flabbergasting that the Universe itself seemed to be saying to them, "I await your instructions. You can be anything you want to be. I will be anything you want me to be."

Hi ho.

◆◆◆

I learned about this Chinese scheme long after Eliza died, and long after I lost all my authority as President of the United States of America. There was nothing I could do with such knowledge by then.

One thing amused me, though: I was told that poor old Western Civilization had provided the Chinese the inspiration to put together such synthetic geniuses. The Chinese got the idea from the American and European scientists who put their heads together during the Second World War, with the single-minded intention of creating an atomic bomb.

Hi ho.

◆◆◆

Chapter 17

❖❖❖❖❖❖❖❖❖❖❖

OUR poor parents had first believed that we were idiots. They had tried to adapt to that. Then they believed that we were geniuses. They had tried to adapt to that. Now they were told that we were dull normals, and they were trying to adapt to that.

As Eliza and I watched through peepholes, they made a pitiful and fog-bound plea for help. They asked Dr. Cordelia Swain Cordiner how they were to harmonize our dullness with the fact that we could converse so learnedly on so many subjects in so many languages.

Dr. Cordiner was razor-keen to enlighten them on

just this point. "The world is full of people who are very clever at seeming much smarter than they really are," she said. "They dazzle us with facts and quotations and foreign words and so on, whereas the truth is that they know almost nothing of use in life as it is really lived. My purpose is to *detect* such people—so that society can be protected from them, and so they can be protected from themselves.

"Your Eliza is a perfect example," she went on. "She has lectured to me on economics and astronomy and music and every other subject you can think of, and yet she can neither read nor write, nor will she ever be able to."

◆◆◆

She said that our case was not a sad one, since there were no big jobs we wished to hold. "They have almost no ambition at all," she said, "so life can't disappoint them. They want only that life as they have known it should go on forever, which is impossible, of course."

Father nodded sadly. "And the boy is the smarter of the two?"

"To the extent he can read and write," said Dr. Cordiner. "He isn't nearly as socially outgoing as his sister. When he is away from her, he becomes as silent as a tomb.

"I suggest that he be sent to some special school, which won't be too demanding academically or too threatening socially, where he can learn to paddle his own canoe."

"Do what?" said Father.

Dr. Cordiner told him again. "Paddle his own canoe," she said.

◆◆◆

Eliza and I should have kicked our way through the wall at that point—should have entered the library ragingly, in an explosion of plaster and laths.

But we had sense enough to know that our power to eavesdrop at will was one of the few advantages we had. So we stole back to our bedrooms, and then burst into the corridor, and came running down the front stairs and across the foyer and into the library, doing something we had never done before. We were sobbing.

We announced that, if anybody tried to part us, we would kill ourselves.

◆◆◆

Dr. Cordiner laughed at this. She told our parents that several of the questions in her tests were designed to detect suicidal tendencies. "I absolutely guarantee you," she said, "that the last thing either one of these two would do would be to commit suicide."

Her saying this so jovially was a tactical mistake on her part, for it caused something in Mother to snap. The atmosphere in the room became electrified as Mother stopped being a weak and polite and credulous doll.

Mother did not say anything at first. But she had

clearly become subhuman in the finest sense. She was a coiled female panther, suddenly willing to tear the throats out of any number of childrearing experts —in defense of her young.

It was the one and only time that she would ever be irrationally committed to being the mother of Eliza and me.

◆◆◆

Eliza and I sensed this sudden jungle alliance telepathically, I think. At any rate, I remember that the damp velvet linings of my sinus cavities were tingling with encouragement.

We left off our crying, which we were no good at doing anyway. Yes, and we made a clear demand which could be satisfied at once. We asked to be tested for intelligence again—as a *pair* this time.

"We want to show you," I said, "how glorious we are when we work together, so that nobody will ever talk about parting us again."

We spoke carefully. I explained who "Betty and Bobby Brown" were. I agreed that they were stupid. I said we had had no experience with hating, and had had trouble understanding that particular human activity whenever we encountered it in books.

"But we are making small beginnings in hating now," said Eliza. "Our hating is strictly limited at this point—to only two people in this Universe: To Betty and Bobby Brown."

◆◆◆

Dr. Cordiner, as it turned out, was a coward, among other things. Like so many cowards, she chose to go on bullying at the worst possible time. She jeered at Eliza's and my request.

"What kind of a world do you think this is?" she said, and so on.

So Mother got up and went over to her, not touching her, and not looking her in the eyes, either. Mother spoke to her throat, and, in a tone between a purr and a growl, she called Dr. Cordiner an "overdressed little sparrow-fart."

◆◆◆

Chapter 18

❖❖❖❖❖❖❖❖❖

So Eliza and I were re-
tested—as a *pair* this time. We sat side-by-side at the
stainless steel table in the tiled diningroom.

We were so happy!

A depersonalized Dr. Cordelia Swain Cordiner ad-
ministered the tests like a robot, while our parents
looked on. She had furnished us with new tests, so
that the challenges would all be fresh.

Before we began, Eliza said to Mother and Father,
"We promise to answer every question correctly."

Which we did.

❖❖❖

What were the questions like? Well, I was poking around the ruins of a school on Forty-sixth Street yesterday, and I was lucky enough to find a whole batch of intelligence tests, all set to go.

I quote:

"A man purchased 100 shares of stock at five dollars a share. If each share rose ten cents the first month, decreased eight cents the second month, and gained three cents the third month, what was the value of the man's investment at the end of the third month?"

Or try this:

"How many digits are there to the left of the decimal place in the square root of 692038.42753?"

Or this:

"A yellow tulip viewed through a piece of blue glass looks what color?"

Or this:

"Why does the Little Dipper appear to turn about the North Star once a day?"

Or this:

"Astronomy is to geology as steeplejack is to what?"

And so on. Hi ho.

❖❖❖

We made good on Eliza's promise of perfection, as I have said.

The only trouble was that the two of us, in the innocent process of checking and rechecking our answers, wound up under the table—with our legs wrapped around each others' necks in scissors grips, and snorting and snuffling into each others' crotches.

When we regained our chairs, Dr. Cordelia Swain Cordiner had fainted, and our parents were gone.

◆◆◆

At ten o'clock the next morning, I was taken by automobile to a school for severely disturbed children on Cape Cod.

◆◆◆

Chapter 19

◆◆◆◆◆◆◆◆◆◆

IT is sundown again. A bird down around Thirty-first Street and Fifth, where there is an Army tank with a tree growing out of its turret, calls out to me. It asks the same question over and over again with piercing clarity.

"Whip poor Will?" it says.

I never call that bird a "whippoorwill," and neither do Melody and Isadore, who follow my lead in naming things. They seldom call Manhattan "Manhattan," for example, or "The Island of Death," which is its common name on the mainland. They do as I do: They call it "Skyscraper National Park," without knowing what the joke is in that, or, with equal humorlessness, "Angkor Wat."

And what they call the bird that asks about whipping when the sun goes down is what Eliza and I called it when we were children. It was a correct name which we had learned from a dictionary.

We treasured the name for the superstitious dread it inspired. The bird became a nightmare creature in a painting by Hieronymus Bosch when we spoke its name. And, whenever we heard its cry, we spoke its name simultaneously. It was almost the only occasion on which we would speak simultaneously.

"The cry of *The Nocturnal Goatsucker*," we would say.

◆◆◆

And now I hear Melody and Isadore saying that, too, in a part of the lobby where I cannot see them. "The cry of the Nocturnal Goatsucker," they say.

◆◆◆

Eliza and I listened to that bird one evening before my departure for Cape Cod.

We had fled the mansion for the privacy of the dank mausoleum of Professor Elihu Roosevelt Swain.

"Whip poor Will?" came the question, from somewhere out under the apple trees.

◆◆◆

106

Even when we put our heads together, we could think of little to say.

I have heard that condemned prisoners often think of themselves as dead people, long before they die. Perhaps that was how our genius felt, knowing that a cruel axeman, so to speak, was about to split it into two nondescript chunks of meat, into Betty and Bobby Brown.

Be that as it may, our hands were busy—which is often the case with the hands of dying people. We had brought what we thought were the best of our writings with us. We rolled them into a cylinder, which we hid in an empty bronze funerary urn.

The urn had been intended for the ashes of the wife of Professor Swain, who had chosen to be buried here in New York, instead. It was encrusted with verdigris.

Hi ho.

❖❖❖

What was on the papers?

A method for squaring circles, I remember—and a utopian scheme for creating artificial extended families in America by issuing everyone a new middle name. All persons with the same middle name would be relatives.

Yes, and there was our critique of Darwin's Theory of Evolution, and an essay on the nature of gravity, which concluded that gravity had surely been a variable in ancient times.

There was a paper, I remember, which argued that teeth should be washed with hot water, just like dishes and pots and pans.

And so on.

◆◆◆

It was Eliza who had thought of hiding the papers in the urn.

It was Eliza who now put the lid in place.

We were not close together when she did it, so what she said was her own invention: "Say goodbye forever to your intelligence, Bobby Brown."

"Goodbye," I said.

◆◆◆

"Eliza—" I said, "so many of the books I've read to you said that love was the most important thing of all. Maybe I should tell you that I love you now."

"Go ahead," she said.

"I love you, Eliza," I said.

She thought about it. "No," she said at last, "I don't like it."

"Why not?" I said.

"It's as though you were pointing a gun at my head," she said. "It's just a way of getting somebody to say something they probably don't mean. What else can I say, or *anybody* say, but, 'I love you, too'?"

"You don't love me?" I said.

"What could anybody love about Bobby Brown?" she said.

◆◆◆

Somewhere outside, out under the apple trees, the Nocturnal Goatsucker asked his question again.

◆◆◆

Chapter 20

◆◆◆◆◆◆◆◆◆

ELIZA did not come down to breakfast the next morning. She remained in her room until I was gone.

Our parents came along with me in their chauffeur-driven Mercedes limousine. I was their child with a future. I could read and write.

And, even as we rolled through the lovely countryside, my forgettery set to work.

It was a protective mechanism against unbearable grief, one which I, as a pediatrician, am persuaded all children have.

Somewhere behind me, it seemed, was a twin sister who was not nearly as smart as I was. She had a name. Her name was Eliza Mellon Swain.

◆◆◆

Yes, and the school year was so structured that none of us ever had to go home. I went to England and France and Germany and Italy and Greece. I went to summer camp.

And it was determined that, while I was surely no genius, and was incapable of originality, I had a better than average mind. I was patient and orderly, and could sort out good ideas from heaps of balderdash.

I was the first child in the history of the school to take College Boards. I did so well that I was invited to come to Harvard. I accepted the invitation, although my voice had yet to change.

And I would now and then be reminded by my parents, who became very proud of me, that somewhere I had a twin sister who was little more than a human vegetable. She was in an expensive institution for people of her sort.

She was only a name.

◆◆◆

Father was killed in an automobile accident during my first year in medical school. He had thought enough of me to name me an executor of his will.

And I was visited in Boston soon after that by a fat and shifty-eyed attorney named Norman Mushari, Jr. He told me what seemed at first to be a rambling and irrelevant story about a woman who had been locked away for many years against her will—in an institution for the feeble-minded.

She had hired him, he said, to sue her relatives and the institution for damages, to gain her release at once, and to recover all inheritances which had been wrongly withheld.

She had a name, which, of course, was Eliza Mellon Swain.

◆◆◆

Chapter 21

◆◆◆◆◆◆◆◆◆

MOTHER would say later of the hospital where we abandoned Eliza to Limbo: "It wasn't a cheap hospital, you know. It cost two hundred dollars a day. And the doctors begged us to stay away, didn't they, Wilbur?"

"I think so, Mother," I said. And then I told the truth: "I forget."

◆◆◆

I was then not only a stupid Bobby Brown, but a conceited one. Though only a first-year medical student with the genitalia of an infant field mouse, I was the master of a great house on Beacon Hill. I was driven to and from school in a Jaguar—and I had already taken to dressing as I would dress when President of the United States, like a medical mountebank during the era of Chester Alan Arthur, say.

There was a party there nearly every night. I would customarily make an appearance of only a few minutes—smoking hashish in a meerschaum pipe, and wearing an emerald-green, watered-silk dressing gown.

A pretty girl came up to me at one of those parties, and she said to me, "You are so ugly, you're the sexiest thing I ever saw."

"I know," I said. "I know, I know."

◆◆◆

Mother visited me a lot on Beacon Hill, where I had a special suite built just for her—and I visited her a lot in Turtle Bay. Yes, and reporters came to question us in both places after Norman Mushari, Jr., got Eliza out of the hospital.

It was a big story.

It was always a big story when multimillionaires mistreated their own relatives.

Hi ho.

◆◆◆

It was embarrassing, and should have been, of course.

We had not seen Eliza yet, and had not been able

to reach her by telephone. Meanwhile, though, she said justly insulting things about us almost every day in the press.

All we had to show reporters was a copy of a telegram we had sent to Eliza, in care of her lawyer, and Eliza's reply to it.

Our telegram said:

"WE LOVE YOU. YOUR MOTHER AND YOUR BROTHER."

Eliza's telegram said this:

"I LOVE YOU TOO. ELIZA."

◆◆◆

Eliza would not allow herself to be photographed. She had her lawyer buy a confessional booth from a church which was being torn down. She sat inside it when she granted interviews for television.

And Mother and I watched those interviews in agony, holding hands.

And Eliza's rowdy contralto had become so unfamiliar to us that we thought there might be an imposter in the booth, but it was Eliza all right.

I remember a television reporter asked her, "How did you spend your time in the hospital, Miss Swain?"

"Singing," she said.

"Singing anything in particular?" he said.

"The same song—over and over again," she said.

"What song was that?" he said.

" 'Some Day My Prince Will Come,' " she told him.

"And did you have some specific prince in mind—as your rescuer?" he said.

"My twin brother," she said. "But he's a swine, of course. He never came."

◆◆◆

Chapter 22

◆◆◆◆◆◆◆◆◆

MOTHER and I surely did not oppose Eliza and her lawyer in any way, so she easily regained control of her wealth. And nearly the first thing she did was to buy half-interest in The New England Patriots professional football team.

◆◆◆

This purchase resulted in more publicity. Eliza would still not come out of the booth for cameras, but Mushari promised the world that she was now wearing a New England Patriots blue and gold jersey in there.

She was asked in this particular interview if she

kept up with current events, to which she replied: "I certainly don't blame the Chinamen for going home."

This had to do with the Republic of China's closing its embassy in Washington. The miniaturization of human beings in China had progressed so far at that point, that their ambassador was only sixty centimeters tall. His farewell was polite and friendly. He said his country was severing relations simply because there was no longer anything going on in the United States which was of any interest to the Chinese at all.

Eliza was asked to say why the Chinamen had been so right.

"What civilized country could be interested in a hell-hole like America," she said, "where everybody takes such lousy care of their own relatives?"

◆◆◆

And then, one day, she and Mushari were seen crossing the Massachusetts Avenue Bridge from Cambridge to Boston on foot. It was a warm and sunny day. Eliza was carrying a parasol. She was wearing the jersey of her football team.

◆◆◆

My God—was that poor girl ever a mess!

She was so bent over that her face was on level with Mushari's—and Mushari was about the size of Napoleon Bonaparte. She was chain smoking. She was coughing her head off.

Mushari was wearing a white suit. He carried a cane. He wore a red rose in his lapel.

And he and his client were soon joined by a friendly crowd, and by newspaper photographers and television crews.

And mother and I watched them on television—in horror, may I say, for the parade was coming ever closer to my house on Beacon Hill.

◆◆◆

"Oh, Wilbur, Wilbur, Wilbur—" said my mother as we watched, "is that really your sister?"

I made a bitter joke—without smiling. "Either your only daughter, Mother, or the sort of anteater known as an *aardvark*," I said.

◆◆◆

Chapter 23

❖❖❖❖❖❖❖❖❖❖

MOTHER was not up to a confrontation with Eliza. She retreated to her suite upstairs. Nor did I want the servants to witness whatever grotesque performance Eliza had in mind—so I sent them to their quarters.

When the doorbell rang, I myself answered the door.

I smiled at the aardvark and the cameras and the crowd. "Eliza! Dear sister! What a pleasant surprise. Come in, come in!" I said.

For form's sake, I made a tentative gesture as though I might touch her. She drew back. "You touch me, Lord Fauntleroy, and I'll bite you, and you'll die of rabies," she said.

◆◆◆

Policemen kept the crowd from following Eliza and Mushari into the house, and I closed the drapes on the windows, so no one could see in.

When I was sure we had privacy, I said to her bleakly, "What brings you here?"

"Lust for your perfect body, Wilbur," she said. She coughed and laughed. "Is dear Mater here, or dear Pater?" She corrected herself. "Oh, dear—dear Pater is dead, isn't he? Or is it dear Mater? It's so hard to tell."

"Mother is in Turtle Bay, Eliza," I lied. Inwardly, I was swooning with sorrow and loathing and guilt. I estimated that her crushed ribcage had the capacity of a box of kitchen matches. The room was beginning to smell like a distillery. Eliza had a problem with alcohol as well. Her skin was bad. She had a complexion like our great-grandmother's steamer trunk.

"Turtle Bay, Turtle Bay," she mused. "Did it ever occur to you, dear Brother, that dear Father was not our Father at all?"

"What do you mean?" I said.

"Perhaps Mother stole from the bed and out of the house on a moonlit night," she said, "and mated with a giant sea turtle in Turtle Bay."

Hi ho.

◆◆◆

"Eliza," I said, "if we're going to discuss family matters, perhaps Mr. Mushari should leave us alone."

121

"Why?" she said. "Normie is the only family I have."

"Now, now—" I said.

"That overdressed sparrow-fart of a mother of yours is surely no relative of mine," she said.

"Now, now—" I said.

"And you don't consider yourself a relative of mine, do you?" she said.

"What can I say?" I said.

"That's why we're visiting you—to hear all the wonderful things you have to say," she said. "You were always the brainy one. I was just some kind of tumor that had to be removed from your side."

◆◆◆

"I never said that," I said.

"Other people said it, and you believed them," she said. "That's worse. You're a Fascist, Wilbur. That's what you are."

"That's absurd," I said.

"Fascists are inferior people who believe it when somebody tells them they're superior," she said.

"Now, now—" I said.

"Then they want everybody else to die," she said.

◆◆◆

"This is getting us nowhere," I said.

"I'm *used* to getting nowhere," she said, "as you may have read in the papers and seen on television."

"Eliza—" I said, "would it help at all for you to

know that Mother will be sick for the rest of our lives about that awful thing we did to you?"

"How could that help?" she said. "That's the dumbest question I ever heard."

❖❖❖

She looped a great arm over the shoulders of Norman Mushari, Jr. "Here's who knows how to help people," she said.

I nodded. "We're grateful to him. We really are."

"He's my mother and father and brother and God, all wrapped up in one," she said. "He gave me the gift of life!

"He said to me, 'Money isn't going to make you feel any better, Sweetheart, but we're going to sue the piss out of your relatives anyway.' "

"Um," I said.

"But it sure helps a hell of a lot more than your expressions of guilt, I must say. Those are just boasts about your own wonderful sensibilities."

She laughed unpleasantly. "But I can see where you and Mother might want to boast about your guilt. After all, it's the only thing you two monkeys ever earned."

Hi ho.

❖❖❖

Chapter 24

◆◆◆◆◆◆◆◆◆◆

I assumed that Eliza had now assaulted my self-respect with every weapon she had. I had somehow survived.

Without pride, with a clinical and cynical sort of interest, I noted that I had a cast-iron character which would repel attacks, apparently, even if I declined to put up defenses of any other kind.

How wrong I was about Eliza's having expended her fury!

Her opening attacks had been aimed merely at exposing the cast iron in my character. She had merely sent out light patrols to cut down the trees and shrubs in front of my character, to strip it of its vines, so to speak.

And now, without my realizing it, the shell of my character stood before her concealed howitzers at nearly point-blank range, as naked and brittle as a Franklin stove.

Hi ho.

◆◆◆

There was a lull. Eliza prowled about my livingroom, looking at my books, which she couldn't read, of course. Then she returned to me, and she cocked her head, and she said, "People get into Harvard Medical School because they can read and write?"

"I worked very hard, Eliza," I said. "It wasn't easy for me. It isn't easy now."

"If Bobby Brown becomes a doctor," she said, "that will be the strongest argument I ever heard for the Christian Scientists."

"I will not be the best doctor there ever was," I said. "I won't be the worst, either."

"You might be a very good man with a gong," she said. She was alluding to recent rumors that the Chinese had had remarkable successes in treating breast cancer with the music of ancient gongs. "You look like a man," she said, "who could hit a gong almost every time."

"Thank you," I said.

"Touch me," she said.

"Pardon me?" I said.

"I'm your own flesh. I'm your sister. Touch me," she said.

"Yes, of course," I said. But my arms seemed queerly paralyzed.

◆◆◆

"Take your time," she said.

"Well—" I said, "since you hate me so—"

"I hate Bobby Brown," she said.

"Since you hate Bobby Brown—" I said.

"And Betty Brown," she said.

"That was so long ago," I said.

"Touch me," she said.

"Oh, Christ, Eliza!" I said. My arms still wouldn't move.

"I'll touch you," she said.

"Whatever you say," I said. I was scared stiff.

"You don't have a heart condition, do you Wilbur?" she said.

"No," I said.

"If I touch you, you promise you won't die?"

"Yes," I said.

"Maybe *I'll* die," she said.

"I hope not," I said.

"Just because I act like I know what's going to happen," she said, "doesn't mean I know what's going to happen. Maybe nothing will happen."

"Maybe," I said.

"I've never seen you so frightened," she said.

"I'm human," I said.

"You want to tell Normie what you're scared about?" she said.

"No," I said.

◆◆◆

Eliza, with her fingertips almost brushing my cheek, quoted from a dirty joke Withers Witherspoon had told another servant when we were children. We had heard it through a wall. The joke had to do with a woman who was wildly responsive during sexual intercourse. In the joke, the woman warned a stranger who was beginning to make love to her.

Eliza passed on the sultry warning to me: "Keep your hat on, Buster. We may wind up miles from here."

◆◆◆

Then she touched me.

We became a single genius again.

◆◆◆

Chapter 25

◆◆◆◆◆◆◆◆◆◆

WE went berserk. It was
only by the Grace of God that we did not tumble out
of the house and into the crowd on Beacon Street.
Some parts of us, of which I had not been at all aware,
of which Eliza had been excruciatingly aware, had
been planning a reunion for a long, long time.

I could no longer tell where I stopped and Eliza
began, or where Eliza and I stopped and the Universe began. It was gorgeous and it was horrible. Yes,
and let this be a measure of the quantity of energy
involved: The orgy went on for five whole nights and
days.

◆◆◆

Eliza and I slept for three days after that. When I at last woke up, I found myself in my own bed. I was being fed intravenously.

Eliza, as I later found out, had been taken to her own home in a private ambulance.

◆◆◆

As for why nobody broke us up or summoned help: Eliza and I captured Norman Mushari, Jr., and poor Mother and the servants—one by one.

I have no memory of doing this.

We tied them to wooden chairs and gagged them, apparently, and set them neatly around the dining-room table.

◆◆◆

We gave them food and water, thank Heavens, or we would have been murderers. We would not let them go to the toilet, however, and fed them nothing but peanut butter and jelly sandwiches. I apparently left the house several times to get more bread and jelly and peanut butter.

And then the orgy would begin again.

◆◆◆

I remember reading out loud to Eliza from books on pediatrics and child psychology and sociology and anthropology, and so on. I had never thrown away any book from any course I had taken.

I remember writhing embraces which alternated with periods of my sitting at my typewriter, with

Eliza beside me. I was typing something with super-human speed.

Hi ho.

◆◆◆

When I came out of my coma, Mushari and my own lawyers had already paid my servants handsomely for the agony they had suffered at the dinner table, and for their silence as to the dreadful things they had seen.

Mother had been released from Massachusetts General Hospital, and was back in bed in Turtle Bay.

◆◆◆

Physically, I had suffered from exhaustion and nothing more.

When I was allowed to rise, however, I was so damaged psychologically that I expected to find everything unfamiliar. If gravity had become variable on that day, as it in fact did many years later, if I had had to crawl about my house on my hands and knees, as I often do now, I would have thought it a highly appropriate response by the Universe to all I had been through.

◆◆◆

But little had changed. The house was tidy.

The books were back in their shelves. A broken thermostat had been replaced. Three diningroom chairs had been sent out for repairs. The diningroom carpet was somewhat piebald, pale spots indicating where stains had been removed.

The one proof that something extraordinary had happened was itself a paradigm of tidiness. It was a manuscript—on a coffee table in the livingroom, where I had typed so furiously during the nightmare.

Eliza and I had somehow written a manual on childrearing.

◆◆◆

Was it any good? Not really. It was only good enough to become, after The Bible and *The Joy of Cooking,* the most popular book of all time.

Hi ho.

◆◆◆

I found it so helpful when I began to practice pediatrics in Vermont that I had it published under a pseudonym, Dr. Eli W. Rockmell, M.D., a sort of garbling of Eliza's and my names.

The publisher thought up the title, which was *So You Went and Had a Baby.*

◆◆◆

During our orgy, though, Eliza and I gave the manuscript a very different title and sort of authorship, which was this:

THE CRY OF THE NOCTURNAL GOATSUCKER
by
BETTY AND BOBBY BROWN

◆◆◆

Chapter 26

◆◆◆◆◆◆◆◆◆

AFTER the orgy, mutual terror kept us apart. I was told by our go-between, Norman Mushari, Jr., that Eliza was even more shattered by the orgy than I had been.

"I almost had to put her away again—" he said, "for good cause this time."

◆◆◆

Machu Picchu, the old Inca capital on the roof of the Andes in Peru, was then becoming a haven for rich people and their parasites, people fleeing social reforms and economic declines, not just in America, but in all parts of the world. There were even some full-sized Chinese there, who had declined to let their children be miniaturized.

And Eliza moved into a condominium down there, to be as far away as possible from me.

◆◆◆

When Mushari came to my house to tell me about Eliza's prospective move to Peru, a week after the orgy, he confessed that he himself had become severely disoriented while tied to a diningroom chair.

"You looked more and more like Frankenstein monsters to me," he said. "I became convinced that there was a switch somewhere in the house that controlled you. I even figured out which switch it was. The minute I untied myself, I ran to it and tore it out by the roots."

It was Mushari who had ripped the thermostat from the wall.

◆◆◆

To demonstrate to me how changed he was, he admitted that he had been wholly motivated by self-interest when he set Eliza free. "I was a bounty-hunter," he said, "finding rich people in mental hospitals who didn't belong there—and setting them free. I left the poor to rot in their dungeons."

"It was a useful service all the same," I said.

"Christ, I don't think so," he said. "Practically every sane person I ever got out of a hospital went insane almost immediately afterwards.

"Suddenly I feel old," he said. "I can't take that any more."

Hi ho.

◆◆◆

Mushari was so shaken by the orgy, in fact, that he turned Eliza's legal and financial affairs over to the same people that Mother and I used.

He came to my attention only once more, two years later, about the time I graduated from medical school—at the bottom of my class, by the way. He had patented an invention of his own. There was a photograph of him and a description of his patent on a business page in *The New York Times*.

There was a national mania for tap-dancing at the time. Mushari had invented taps which could be glued to the soles of shoes, and then peeled off again. A person could carry the taps in little plastic bags in a pocket or purse, according to Mushari, and put them on only when it was time to tap-dance.

◆◆◆

Chapter 27

❖❖❖❖❖❖❖❖❖❖❖

I never saw Eliza's face again after the orgy. I heard her voice only twice more—once when I graduated from medical school, and again when I was President of the United States of America, and she had been dead for a long, long time.

Hi ho.

❖❖❖

When Mother planned a graduation party for me at the Ritz in Boston, across from the Public Gardens, she and I never dreamed that Eliza would somehow hear of it, and would come all the way from Peru.

My twin never wrote or telephoned. Rumors about her were as vague as those coming from China. She was drinking too much, we had heard. She had taken up golf.

◆◆◆

I was having a wonderful time at my party, when a bellboy came to tell me I was wanted outside—not just in the lobby, but in the balmy, moonlit night outdoors. Eliza was the farthest thing from my mind.

My guess, as I followed the bellboy, was that there was a Rolls-Royce from my mother parked outside.

I was reassured by the servile manner and uniform of my guide. I was also giddy with champagne. I did not hesitate to follow as he led me across Arlington Street and then into the enchanted forest, into the Public Gardens on the other side.

He was a fraud. He was not a bellboy at all.

◆◆◆

Deeper and deeper we went into the trees. And in every clearing we came to, I expected to see my Rolls-Royce.

But he brought me to a statue instead. It depicted an old-fashioned doctor, dressed much as it amused me to dress. He was melancholy but proud. He held a sleeping youth in his arms.

As the inscription in the moonlight told me, this was a monument to the first use of anaesthetics in surgery in the United States, which took place in Boston.

◆◆◆

I had been aware of a clattering whir somewhere in the city, over Commonwealth Avenue perhaps. But I had not identified it as a hovering helicopter.

But now the bogus bellhop, who was really an Inca servant of Eliza's, fired a magnesium flare into the air.

Everything touched by that unnatural dazzle became statuary—lifeless and exemplary, and weighing tons.

The helicopter materialized directly over us, itself made allegorical, transformed into a terrible mechanical angel by the glare of the flare.

Eliza was up there with a bullhorn.

◆◆◆

It seemed possible to me that she might shoot me from there, or hit me with a bag of excrement. She had traveled all the way from Peru to deliver one-half of a Shakespearean sonnet.

"Listen!" she said. "Listen!" she said. And then she said, "Listen!" again.

The flare was meanwhile dying nearby—its parachute snagged in a treetop.

Here is what Eliza said to me, and to the neighborhood:

"O! how thy worth with manners may I sing,
"When thou art all the better part of me?
"What can mine own praise to mine own self bring?

"And what is't but mine own when I praise
thee?

"Even for this let us divided live,

"And our dear love lose name of single one,

"That by this separation I may give

"That due to thee, which thou deserv'st alone."

◆◆◆

I called up to her through my cupped hands. "Eliza!"
I said. And then I shouted something daring, and
something I genuinely felt for the first time in my
life.

"Eliza! I love you!" I said.

All was darkness now.

"Did you hear me, Eliza?" I said. "I *love* you! I
really love you!"

"I heard you," she said. "Nobody should ever say
that to anybody."

"I mean it," I said.

"Then I will say in turn something that I really
mean, my brother—my twin."

"What is it?" I said.

She said this: "God guide the hand and mind of Dr.
Wilbur Rockefeller Swain."

◆◆◆

And then the helicopter flew away.

Hi ho.

◆◆◆

Chapter 28

◆◆◆◆◆◆◆◆◆◆◆

I returned to the Ritz, laughing and crying—a two-meter Neanderthaler in a ruffled shirt and a robin's-egg blue velvet tuxedo.

There was a crowd of people who were curious about the brief supernova in the east, and about the voice which had spoken from Heaven of separation and love. I pressed past them and into the ballroom, leaving it to private detectives stationed at the door to turn back the following crowd.

The guests at my party were only now beginning to hear hints that something marvelous had happened outside. I went to Mother, to tell her what Eliza had done. I was puzzled to find her talking to a nondescript, middle-aged stranger, dressed, like the detectives, in a cheap business suit.

Mother introduced him as "Dr. Mott." He was, of course, the doctor who had looked after Eliza and me for so long in Vermont. He was in Boston on business, and, as luck would have it, staying at the Ritz.

I was so full of news and champagne, though, that I did not know or care who he was. And, having said my bit to Mother, I told Dr. Mott that it had been nice to meet him, and I hurried on to other parts of the room.

◆◆◆

When I got back to Mother in about an hour, Dr. Mott had departed. She told me again who he was. I expressed pro forma regrets at not having spent more time with him. She gave me a note from him, which she said was his graduation present to me.

It was written on Ritz stationery. It said simply this:

" 'If you can do no good, at least do no harm.' Hippocrates."

◆◆◆

Yes, and when I converted the mansion in Vermont into a clinic and small children's hospital, and also my permanent home, I had those words chipped in stone over the front door. But they so troubled my patients and their parents that I had them chipped away again. The words seemed a confession of weakness and indecision to them, a suggestion that they might as well have stayed away.

141

I continued to carry the words in my head, however, and in fact did little harm. And the intellectual center of gravity for my practice was a single volume which I locked into a safe each night—the bound manuscript of the child-rearing manual Eliza and I had written during our orgy on Beacon Hill.

Somehow, we had put *everything* in there.

And the years flew by.

◆◆◆

Somewhere in there I married an equally wealthy woman, actually a third cousin of mine, whose maiden name was Rose Aldrich Ford. She was very unhappy, because I did not love her, and because I would never take her anywhere. I have never been good at loving. We had a child, Carter Paley Swain, whom I also failed to love. Carter was normal, and completely uninteresting to me. He was somehow like a summer squash on the vine—featureless and watery, and merely growing larger all the time.

After our divorce, he and his mother bought a condominium in the same building with Eliza, down in Machu Picchu, Peru. I never heard from them again —even when I became President of the United States.

And the time flew.

◆◆◆

I woke up one morning to find that I was almost fifty years old! Mother had moved in with me in Vermont.

She sold her house in Turtle Bay. She was feeble and afraid.

She talked a good deal about Heaven to me.

I knew nothing at all about the subject then. I assumed that when people were dead they were dead.

"I know your father is waiting for me with open arms," she said, "and my Mommy and Daddy, too."

She was right about that, it turned out. Waiting around for more people is just about all there is for people in Heaven to do.

◆◆◆

The way Mother described Heaven, it sounded like a golf course in Hawaii, with manicured fairways and greens running down to a lukewarm ocean.

I twitted her only lightly about wanting that sort of Paradise. "It sounds like a place where people would drink a lot of lemonade," I said.

"I love lemonade," she replied.

◆◆◆

Chapter 29

◆◆◆◆◆◆◆◆◆

MOTHER talked toward the end, too, about how much she hated unnatural things—synthetic flavors and fibers and plastics and so on. She loved silk and cotton and linen and wool and leather, she said, and clay and glass and stone. She loved horses and sailboats, too, she said.

"They're all coming back, Mother," I said, which was true.

My hospital itself had twenty horses by then—and wagons and carts and carriages and sleighs. I had a horse of my own, a great Clydesdale. Golden feathers hid her hooves. "Budweiser" was her name.

Yes, and the harbors of New York and Boston and San Francisco were forests of masts again, I'd heard. It had been quite some time since I'd seen them.

◆◆◆

Yes, and I found the hospitality of my mind to fantasy pleasantly increased as machinery died and communications from the outside world became more and more vague.

So I was unsurprised one night, after having tucked Mother in bed, to enter my own bedroom with a lighted candle, and to find a Chinese man the size of my thumb sitting on my mantelpiece. He was wearing a quilted blue jacket and trousers and cap.

As far as I was able to determine afterwards, he was the first official emissary from the People's Republic of China to the United States of America in more than twenty-five years.

◆◆◆

During the same period, not a single foreigner who got inside China, so far as I know, ever returned from there.

So "going to China" became a widespread euphemism for committing suicide.

Hi ho.

◆◆◆

My little visitor motioned for me to come closer, so he would not have to shout. I presented one ear to him. It must have been a horrible sight—the tunnel with all the hair and bits of wax inside.

He told me that he was a roving ambassador, and had been chosen for the job because of his visibility to foreigners. He was much, much larger, he said, than an average Chinese.

"I thought you people had no interest in us any more," I said.

He smiled. "That was a foolish thing for us to say, Dr. Swain," he said. "We apologize."

"You mean that we know things that you don't know?" I said.

"Not quite," he said. "I mean that you *used* to know things that we don't know."

"I can't imagine what those things would be," I said.

"Naturally not," he said. "I will give you a hint: I bring you greetings from your twin sister in Machu Picchu, Dr. Swain."

"That's not much of a hint," I said.

"I wish very much to see the papers you and your sister put so many years ago into the funeral urn in the mausoleum of Professor Elihu Roosevelt Swain," he said.

◆◆◆

It turned out that the Chinese had sent an expedition to Machu Picchu—to recover, if they could, certain lost secrets of the Incas. Like my visitor, they were oversize for Chinese.

Yes, and Eliza approached them with a proposition. She said she knew where there were secrets which were as good or better than anything the Incas had had.

"If what I say turns out to be true," she told them, "I want you to reward me—with a trip to your colony on Mars."

◆◆◆

He said that his name was Fu Manchu.

◆◆◆

I asked him how he had got to my mantelpiece.

"The same way we get to Mars," he replied.

◆◆◆

Chapter 30

❖❖❖❖❖❖❖❖

I agreed to take Fu Manchu out to the mausoleum. I put him in my breast pocket.

I felt very inferior to him. I was sure he had the power of life and death over me, as small as he was. Yes, and he knew so much more than I did—even about medicine, even about myself, perhaps. He made me feel immoral, too. It was greedy for me to be so big. My supper that night could have fed a thousand men his size.

❖❖❖

The exterior doors to the mausoleum had been welded shut. So Fu Manchu and I had to enter the secret passageways, the alternative universe of my childhood, and come up through the mausoleum's floor.

As I made our way through cobwebs, I asked him about the Chinese use of gongs in the treatment of cancer.

"We are way beyond that now," he said.

"Maybe it is something we could still use here," I said.

"I'm sorry—" he said from my pocket, "but your civilization, so-called, is much too primitive. You could never understand."

"Um," I said.

❖❖❖

He answered all my questions that way—saying, in effect, that I was too dumb to understand anything.

❖❖❖

When we got to the underside of the stone trapdoor to the mausoleum, I had trouble heaving it open.

"Put your shoulder into it," he said, and, "Tap it with a brick," and so on.

His advice was so simple-minded, that I concluded that the Chinese knew little more about dealing with gravity than I did at the time.

Hi ho.

◆◆◆

The door finally opened, and we ascended into the mausoleum. I must have been even more frightful than usual to look at. I was swaddled in cobwebs from head to toe.

I removed Fu Manchu from my pocket, and, at his request, I placed him on top of the lead casket of Professor Elihu Roosevelt Swain.

I had only one candle for illumination. But Fu Manchu now produced from his attaché case a tiny box. It filled the chamber with a light as brilliant as the flare that had lit Eliza's and my reunion in Boston —so long ago.

He asked me to take the papers from the urn, which I did. They were perfectly preserved.

"This is bound to be trash," I said.

"To you, perhaps," he said. He asked me to flatten out the papers and spread them over the casket, which I did.

"How could we know when we were children something not known even today to the Chinese?" I said.

"Luck," he said. He began to stroll across the papers, in his tiny black and white basketball shoes, pausing here and there to take pictures of something he had read. He seemed especially interested in our essay on gravity—or so it seems to me now, with the benefit of hindsight.

◆◆◆

He was satisfied at last. He thanked me for my cooperation, and told me that he would now dematerialize and return to China.

"Did you find anything at all valuable?" I asked him.

He smiled. "A ticket to Mars for a rather large Caucasian lady in Peru," he replied.

Hi ho.

◆◆◆

Chapter 31

◆◆◆◆◆◆◆◆◆◆

THREE weeks later, on the morning of my fiftieth birthday, I rode my horse Budweiser down into the hamlet—to pick up the mail.

There was a note from Eliza. It said only this: "Happy birthday to us! Going to China!"

That message was two weeks old, according to the postmark. There was fresher news in the same mail. "Regret to inform you that your sister died on Mars in an avalanche." It was signed, "Fu Manchu."

◆◆◆

I read those tragic notes while standing on the old wooden porch of the post office, in the shadow of the little church next door.

An extraordinary feeling came over me, which I first thought to be psychological in origin, the first rush of grief. I seemed to have taken root on the porch. I could not pick up my feet. My features, moreover, were being dragged downward like melting wax.

The truth was that the force of gravity had increased tremendously.

There was a great crash in the church. The steeple had dropped its bell.

Then I went right through the porch, and was slammed to the earth beneath it.

♦♦♦

In other parts of the world, of course, elevator cables were snapping, airplanes were crashing, ships were sinking, motor vehicles were breaking their axles, bridges were collapsing, and on and on.

It was terrible.

♦♦♦

Chapter 32

✦✦✦✦✦✦✦✦✦✦

THAT first ferocious jolt of heavy gravity lasted less than a minute, but the world would never be the same again.

I dazedly climbed out from under the post office porch when it was over. I gathered up my mail.

Budweiser was dead. She had tried to remain standing. Her insides had fallen out.

✦✦✦

I must have suffered something like shell shock. People were crying for help there in the hamlet, and I was the only doctor. But I simply walked away.

I remember wandering under the family apple trees.

154

I remember stopping at the family cemetery, and gravely opening an envelope from the Eli Lilly Company, a pharmaceutical house. Inside were a dozen sample pills, the color and size of lentils.

The accompanying literature, which I read with great care, explained that the trade name for the pills was "tri-benzo-Deportamil." The "Deport" part of the name had reference to good deportment, to socially acceptable behavior.

The pills were a treatment for the socially unacceptable symptoms of Tourette's Disease, whose sufferers involuntarily spoke obscenities and made insulting gestures no matter where they were.

In my disoriented state, it seemed very important that I take two of the pills immediately, which I did.

Two minutes passed, and then my whole being was flooded with contentment and confidence such as I had never felt before.

Thus began an addiction which was to last for nearly thirty years.

Hi ho.

◆◆◆

It was a miracle that no one in my hospital died. The beds and wheelchairs of some of the heavier children had broken. One nurse crashed through the trapdoor which had once been hidden by Eliza's bed. She broke both legs.

Mother, thank God, slept through it all.

When she woke up, I was standing at the foot of

her bed. She told me again about how much she hated unnatural things.

"I know, Mother," I said. "I couldn't agree with you more. Back to Nature," I said.

◆◆◆

I do not know to this day whether that awful jolt of gravity was Nature, or whether it was an experiment by the Chinese.

I thought at the time that there was a connection between the jolt and Fu Manchu's photographing of Eliza's and my essay on gravity.

Yes, and, coked to the ears on tri-benzo-Deportamil, I fetched all our papers from the mausoleum.

◆◆◆

The paper on gravity was incomprehensible to me. Eliza and I were perhaps ten thousand times as smart when we put our heads together as when we were far apart.

Our Utopian scheme for reorganizing America into thousands of artificial extended families, however, was clear. Fu Manchu had found it ridiculous, incidentally.

"This is truly the work of children," he'd said.

◆◆◆

I found it absorbing. It said that there was nothing new about artificial extended families in America. Physicians felt themselves related to other physicians, lawyers to lawyers, writers to writers, athletes to athletes, politicians to politicians, and so on.

Eliza and I said these were bad sorts of extended families, however. They excluded children and old people and housewives, and losers of every description. Also: Their interests were usually so specialized as to seem nearly insane to outsiders.

"An ideal extended family," Eliza and I had written so long ago, "should give proportional representation to all sorts of Americans, according to their numbers. The creation of ten thousand such families, say, would provide America with ten thousand parliaments, so to speak, which would discuss sincerely and expertly what only a few hypocrites now discuss with passion, which is the welfare of all mankind."

◆◆◆

My reading was interrupted by my head nurse, who came in to tell me that our frightened young patients had all gotten to sleep at last.

I thanked her for the good news. And then I heard myself tell her casually, "Oh—and I want you to write to the Eli Lilly Company, in Indianapolis, and order two thousand doses of a new drug of theirs called 'tri-benzo-Deportamil.' "

Hi ho.

◆◆◆

Chapter 33

◆◆◆◆◆◆◆◆◆◆

MOTHER died two weeks after that.

Gravity would not trouble us again for another twenty years.

And time flew. Time was a blurry bird now—made indistinct by ever-increasing dosages of tri-benzo-Deportamil.

◆◆◆

Somewhere in there, I closed my hospital, gave up medicine entirely, and was elected United States Senator from Vermont.

And time flew.

I found myself running for President one day. My

valet pinned a campaign button to the lapel of my
claw-hammer coat. It bore the slogan which would
win the election for me:

I appeared here in New York only once during that
campaign. I spoke from the steps of the Public Library at Forty-second and Fifth. This island was by
then a sleepy seaside resort. It had never recovered
from that first jolt of gravity, which had stripped its
buildings of their elevators, and had flooded its tunnels, and had buckled all but one bridge, which was
the Brooklyn Bridge.

Now gravity had started to turn mean again. It was
no longer a jolting experience. If the Chinese were
indeed in charge of it, they had learned how to increase or decrease it gradually, wishing to cut down
on injuries and property damage, perhaps. It was as
majestically graceful as the tides now.

◆◆◆

When I spoke from the library steps, the gravity was heavy. So I chose to sit in a chair while speaking. I was cold sober, but I lolled in the chair like a drunken English squire from olden times.

My audience, which was composed mostly of retired people, actually lay down on Fifth Avenue, which the police had blocked off, but where there would have been hardly any traffic anyway. Somewhere over on Madison Avenue, perhaps, there was a small explosion. The island's useless skyscrapers were being quarried.

◆◆◆

I spoke of American loneliness. It was the only subject I needed for victory, which was lucky. It was the only subject I had.

It was a shame, I said, that I had not come along earlier in American history with my simple and workable anti-loneliness plan. I said that all the damaging excesses of Americans in the past were motivated by loneliness rather than a fondness for sin.

An old man crawled up to me afterwards and told me how he used to buy life insurance and mutual funds and household appliances and automobiles and so on, not because he liked them or needed them, but because the salesman seemed to promise to be his relative, and so on.

"I had no relatives and I needed relatives," he said.

"Everybody does," I said.

He told me he had been a drunk for a while, trying

to make relatives out of people in bars. "The bartender would be kind of a father, you know—" he said. "And then all of a sudden it was closing time."

"I know," I said. I told him a half-truth about myself which had proved to be popular on the campaign trail. "I used to be so lonesome," I said, "that the only person I could share my innermost thoughts with was a horse named 'Budweiser.'"

And I told him how Budweiser had died.

◆◆◆

During this conversation, I would bring my hand to my mouth again and again, seeming to stifle exclamations and so on. I was actually popping tiny green pills into my mouth. They were outlawed by then, and no longer manufactured. I had perhaps a bushel of them back in the Senate Office Building.

They accounted for my unflagging courtesy and optimism, and perhaps for my failure to age as quickly as other men. I was seventy years old, but I had the vigor of a man half that age.

I had even picked up a pretty new wife, Sophie Rothschild Swain, who was only twenty-three.

◆◆◆

"If you get elected, and I get issued all these new artificial relatives—" said the man. He paused. "How many did you say?"

"Ten thousand brothers and sisters," I told him. "One-hundred and ninety-thousand cousins."

"Isn't that' an awful lot?" he said.

"Didn't we just agree we need all the relatives we can get in a country as big and clumsy as ours?" I said. "If you ever go to Wyoming, say, won't it be a comfort to you to know you have many relatives there?"

He thought that over. "Well, yes—I expect," he said at last.

"As I said in my speech:" I told him, "your new middle name would consist of a noun, the name of a flower or fruit or nut or vegetable or legume, or a bird or a reptile or a fish, or a mollusk, or a gem or a mineral or a chemical element—connected by a hypen to a number between one and twenty." I asked him what his name was at the present time.

"Elmer Glenville Grasso," he said.

"Well," I said, "you might become Elmer Uranium-3 Grasso, say. Everybody with Uranium as a part of their middle name would be your cousin."

"That brings me back to my first question," he said. "What if I get some artificial relative I absolutely can't stand?"

◆◆◆

"What is so novel about a person's having a relative he can't stand?" I asked him. "Wouldn't you say that sort of thing has been going on now for perhaps a million years, Mr. Grasso?"

And then I said a very obscene thing to him. I am not inclined toward obscenities, as this book itself demonstrates. In all my years of public life, I had never said an off-color thing to the American people.

So it was terrifically effective when I at last spoke coarsely. I did so in order to make memorable how nicely scaled to average human beings my new social scheme would be.

Mr. Grasso was not the first to hear the startling rowdy-isms. I had even used them on radio. There was no such thing as television any more.

"Mr. Grasso," I said, "I personally will be very disappointed, if you do not say to artificial relatives you hate, after I am elected, 'Brother or Sister or Cousin,' as the case may be, 'why don't you take a flying fuck at a rolling doughnut? Why don't you take a flying fuck at the moooooooooooooon?' "

◆◆◆

"You know what relatives you say that to are going to do, Mr. Grasso?" I went on. "They're going to go home and try to figure out how to be better relatives!"

◆◆◆

"And consider how much better off you will be, if the reforms go into effect, when a beggar comes up to you and asks for money," I went on.

"I don't understand," said the man.

"Why," I said, "you say to that beggar, 'What's your middle name?' And he will say 'Oyster-19' or 'Chickadee-1,' or 'Hollyhock-13,' or some such thing.

"And you can say to him, 'Buster—I happen to be

a Uranium-3. You have one hundred and ninety thousand cousins and ten thousand brothers and sisters. You're not exactly alone in this world. I have relatives of my own to look after. So why don't you take a flying fuck at a rolling doughnut? Why don't you take a flying fuck at the moooooooooooon?' "

◆◆◆

Chapter 34

THE fuel shortage was so severe when I was elected, that the first stiff problem I faced after my inauguration was where to get enough electricity to power the computers which would issue the new middle names.

I ordered horses and soldiers and wagons of the ramshackle Army I had inherited from my predecessor to haul tons of papers from the National Archives to the powerhouse. These documents were all from the Administration of Richard M. Nixon, the only President who was ever forced to resign.

◆◆◆

I myself went to the Archives to watch. I spoke to the soldiers and a few passers-by from the steps there. I said that Mr. Nixon and his associates had been unbalanced by loneliness of an especially virulent sort.

"He promised to bring us together, but tore us apart instead," I said. "Now, hey presto!, he will bring us together after all."

I posed for photographs beneath the inscription on the facade of the Archives, which said this:

"THE PAST IS PROLOGUE."

"They were not basically criminals," I said. "But they yearned to partake of the brotherhood they saw in Organized Crime."

◆◆◆

"So many crimes committed by lonesome people in Government are concealed in this place," I said, "that the inscription might well read, 'Better a Family of Criminals than No Family at All.'

"I think we are now marking the end of the era of such tragic monkeyshines. The Prologue is over, friends and neighbors and relatives. Let the main body of our noble work begin.

"Thank you," I said.

◆◆◆

There were no large newspapers or national magazines to print my words. The huge printing plants had all shut down—for want of fuel. There were no microphones. There were just the people there.

Hi ho.

I passed out a special decoration to the soldiers, to commemorate the occasion. It consisted of a pale blue ribbon from which depended a plastic button.

I explained, only half-jokingly, that the ribbon represented "The Bluebird of Happiness." And the button was inscribed with these words, of course:

◆◆◆

Chapter 35

^{❖❖❖❖❖❖❖❖❖}

IT is mid-morning here
in Skyscraper National Park. The gravity is balmy,
but Melody and Isadore will not work on the baby's
pyramid today. We will have a picnic on top of the
building instead. The young people are being so
companionable with me because my birthday is only
two days away now. What fun!

There is nothing they love more than a birthday!

Melody plucks a chicken which a slave of Vera
Chipmunk-17 Zappa brought to us this morning. The
slave also brought two loaves of bread and two liters
of creamy beer. He pantomimed how nourishing he

was being to us. He pressed the bases of the two beer bottles to his nipples, pretending that he had breasts that gave creamy beer.

We laughed. We clapped our hands.

◆◆◆

Melody tosses pinches of feathers skyward. Because of the mild gravity, it appears that she is a white witch. Each snap of her fingers produces butterflies.

I have an erection. So does Isadore. So does every male.

◆◆◆

Isadore sweeps the lobby with a broom he has made of twigs. He sings one of the only two songs he knows. The other song is "Happy Birthday to You." Yes, and he is tone-deaf, too, so he drones.

> "Row, row, row your boat," he drones,
> "Gently down the stream.
> "Merrily, merrily, merrily, merrily—
> "Life is but a dream."

◆◆◆

Yes, and I now remember a day in the dream of my life, far upstream from now, in which I received a chatty letter from the President of my country, who happened to be me. Like any other citizen, I had been waiting on pins and needles to learn from the computers what my new middle name would be.

My President congratulated me on my new middle name. He asked me to use it as a regular part of my signature, and on my mailbox and letterheads and in directories, and so on. He said that the name was selected at immaculate random, and was not intended as a comment on my character or my appearance or my past.

He offered deceptively homely, almost inane examples of how I might serve artificial relatives: By watering their houseplants while they were away; by taking care of their babies so they could get out of the house for an hour or two; by telling them the name of a truly painless dentist; by mailing a letter for them; by keeping them company on a scary visit to a doctor; by visiting them in a jail or a hospital; by keeping them company at a scary picture show.

Hi ho.

◆◆◆

I was enchanted by my new middle name, by the way. I ordered that the Oval Office of the White House be painted pale yellow immediately, in celebration of my having become a Daffodil.

And, as I was telling my private secretary, Hortense Muskellunge-13 McBundy, to have the place repainted, a dishwasher from the White House kitchen appeared in her office. He was bent on a very shy errand, indeed. He was so embarrassed that he choked every time he tried to speak.

When he at last managed to articulate his message, I embraced him. He had come out of the steamy depths to tell me ever-so-bravely that he, too, was a *Daffodil-11*.

"My brother," I said.

◆◆◆

Chapter 36

✦✦✦✦✦✦✦✦✦✦

WAS there no substantial opposition to the new social scheme? Why, of course there was. And, as Eliza and I had predicted, my enemies were so angered by the idea of artificial extended families that they constituted a polyglot artificial extended family of their own.

They had campaign buttons, too, which they went on wearing long after I was elected. It was inevitable what those buttons said, to wit:

◆◆◆

I had to laugh, even when my own wife, the former Sophie Rothschild, took to wearing a button like that.

Hi ho.

◆◆◆

Sophie was furious when she received a form letter from her President, who happened to be me, which instructed her to stop being a *Rothschild*. She was to become a *Peanut-3* instead.

Again: I am sorry, but I had to laugh.

◆◆◆

Sophie smouldered about it for several weeks. And then she came crawling into the Oval Office on an afternoon of particularly heavy gravity—to tell me she hated me.

I was not stung.

173

As I have already said, I was fully aware that I was not the sort of lumber out of which happy marriages were made.

"I honestly did not think you would go this far, Wilbur," she said. "I knew you were crazy, and that your sister was crazy, too. But I did not believe you would go this far."

◆◆◆

Sophie did not have to look up at me. I, too, was on the floor—prone, with my chin resting on a pillow. I was reading a fascinating report of a thing that had happened in Urbana, Illinois.

I did not give her my undivided attention, so she said, "What is it you're reading that is so much more interesting than me?"

"Well—" I said, "for many years, I was the last American to have spoken to a Chinese. That's not true any more. A delegation of Chinese paid a call to the widow of a physicist in Urbana—about three weeks ago."

Hi ho.

◆◆◆

"I certainly don't want to waste your valuable time," she said. "You're certainly closer to Chinamen than you ever were to me."

I had given her a wheelchair for Christmas—to use around the White House on days of heavy gravity. I asked her why she didn't use it. "It makes me very sad," I said, "to have you go around on all-fours."

"I'm a *Peanut* now," she said. *"Peanuts* live very close to the ground. *Peanuts* are famous for being low. They are the cheapest of the cheap, and the lowest of the low."

◆◆◆

That early in the game, I thought it was crucial the people not be allowed to change their Government-issue middle names. I was wrong to be so rigid about that. All sorts of name-changing goes on now—here on the Island of Death and everywhere. I can't see that any harm is done.

But I was severe with Sophie. "You want to be an *Eagle* or a *Diamond,* I suppose," I said.

"I want to be a *Rothschild,*" she said.

"Then perhaps you should go to Machu Picchu," I said. That was where most of her blood relatives had gone.

◆◆◆

"Are you really so sadistic," she said, "that you will make me prove my love by befriending strangers who are now crawling out from damp rocks like earwigs? Like centipedes? Like slugs? Like worms?"

"Now, now," I said.

"When was the last time you took a look at the freak show outside the fence?" she said.

The perimeter of the White House grounds, just outside the fence, was infested daily with persons claiming to be artificial relatives of Sophie or me.

There were twin male midgets out there, I remember, holding a banner that said "Flower Power."

There was a woman, I remember, who wore an Army field jacket over a purple evening dress. On her head was an old-fashioned leather aviator's helmet, goggles and all. She had a placard on the end of a stick. "Peanut Butter," it said.

◆◆◆

"Sophie——" I said, "that is not the general American population out there. And you are not mistaken when you say that they have crawled out from under damp rocks—like centipedes and earwigs and worms. They have never had a friend or a relative. They have had to believe all their lives that they were perhaps sent to the wrong Universe, since no one has ever bid them welcome or given them anything to do."

"I hate them," she said.

"Go ahead," I said. "There's very little harm in that, as far as I know."

"I did not think you would go this far, Wilbur," she said. "I thought you would be satisfied with being President. I did not think you would go this far."

"Well," I said, "I'm glad I did. And I am glad we have those people outside the fence to think about, Sophie. They are frightened hermits who have been tempted out from under their damp rocks by humane new laws. They are dazedly seeking brothers and sisters and cousins which their President has suddenly given to them from their nation's social treasure, which was until now untapped."

"You are insane," she said.

"Very likely," I replied. "But it will not be an hallucination when I see those people outside the fence find each other, if no one else."

"They deserve each other," she said.

"Exactly," I said. "And they deserve something else which is going to happen to them, now that they have the courage to speak to strangers. You watch, Sophie. The simple experience of companionship is going to allow them to climb the evolutionary ladder in a matter of hours or days, or weeks at most.

"It will not be an hallucination, Sophie," I said, "when I see them become human beings, after having been for so many years, as you say, Sophie— centipedes and slugs and earwigs and worms."

Hi ho.

◆◆◆

Chapter 37

◆◆◆◆◆◆◆◆◆◆◆

SOPHIE divorced me, of course, and skedaddled with her jewelry and furs and paintings and gold bricks, and so on, to a condominium in Machu Picchu, Peru.

Almost the last thing I said to her, I think, was this: "Can't you at least wait until we compile the family directories? You're sure to find out that you're related to many distinguished women and men."

"I already *am* related to many distinguished women and men," she replied. "Goodbye."

◆◆◆

In order to compile and publish the family directories, we had to haul more papers from the National Archives to the powerhouse. I selected files from the Presidencies of Ulysses Simpson Grant and Warren Gamaliel Harding this time.

We could not provide every citizen with directories of his or her own. It was all we could do to ship a complete set to every State House, town and City Hall, police department, and public library in the land.

◆◆◆

One greedy thing I did: Before Sophie left me, I asked that we be sent Daffodil and Peanut directories all our own. And I have a Daffodil Directory right here in the Empire State Building right now. Vera Chipmunk-5 Zappa gave it to me for my birthday last year. It is a first edition—the only edition ever published.

And I learn from it again that among my new relatives at that time were Clarence Daffodil-11 Johnson, the Chief of Police of Batavia, New York, and Muhammad Daffodil-11 X, the former Light-Heavyweight Boxing Champion of the World, and Maria Daffodil-11 Tcherkassky, the Prima Ballerina of the Chicago Opera Ballet.

◆◆◆

I am glad, in a way, incidentally, that Sophie never saw her family directory. The Peanuts really did seem to be a ground-hugging bunch.

The most famous Peanut I can now recall was a minor Roller Derby star.

Hi ho.

◆◆◆

Yes, and after the Government provided the directories, Free Enterprise produced family newspapers. Mine was *The Daffy-nition.* Sophie's, which continued to arrive at the White House long after she had left me, was *The Goober Gossip.* Vera told me the other day that the *Chipmunk* paper used to be *The Woodpile.*

Relatives asked for work or investment capital, or offered things for sale in the classified ads. The news columns told of triumphs by various relatives, and warned against others who were child molesters or swindlers and so on. There were lists of relatives who could be visited in various hospitals and jails.

There were editorials calling for family health insurance programs and sports teams and so on. There was one interesting essay, I remember, either in *The Daffy-nition* or *The Goober Gossip,* which said that families with high moral standards were the best maintainers of law and order, and that police departments could be expected to fade away.

"If you know of a relative who is engaged in criminal acts," it concluded, "don't call the police. Call ten more relatives."

And so on.

◆◆◆

Vera told me that the motto of *The Woodpile* used to be this: "A Good Citizen is a Good Family Woman or a Good Family Man."

◆◆◆

As the new families began to investigate themselves, some statistical freaks were found. Almost all *Pachysandras*, for example, could play a musical instrument, or at least sing in tune. Three of them were conductors of major symphony orchestras. The widow in Urbana who had been visited by Chinese was a *Pachysandra*. She supported herself and her son by giving piano lessons out there.

Watermelons, on the average, were a kilogram heavier than members of any other family.

Three-quarters of all *Sulfurs* were female.

And on and on.

As for my own family: There was an extraordinary concentration of Daffodils in and around Indianapolis. My family paper was published out there, and its masthead boasted, "Printed in Daffodil City, U.S.A."

Hi ho.

◆◆◆

Family clubhouses appeared. I personally cut the ribbon at the opening of the Daffodil Club here in Manhattan—on Forty-third Street, right off Fifth Avenue.

This was a thought-provoking experience for me, even though I was sedated by tri-benzo-Deportamil. I had once belonged to another club, and to another sort of artificial extended family, too, on the very same premises. So had my father, and both my grandfathers, and all four of my great grandfathers.

Once the building had been a haven for men of power and wealth, and well-advanced into middle age.

Now it teemed with mothers and children, with old people playing checkers or chess or dreaming, with younger adults taking dancing lessons or bowling on the duckpin alleys, or playing the pinball machines.

I had to laugh.

◆◆◆

Chapter 38

◆◆◆◆◆◆◆◆◆◆◆

IT was on that particular visit to Manhattan that I saw my first "Thirteen Club." There were dozens of such raffish establishments in Chicago, I had heard. Now Manhattan had one of its own.

Eliza and I had not anticipated that all the people with "13" in their middle names would naturally band together almost immediately, to form the largest family of all.

And I certainly got a taste of my own medicine when I asked a guard on the door of the Manhattan Thirteen Club if I could come in and have a look around. It was very dark in there.

"All due respect, Mr. President," he said to me, "but are you a *Thirteen,* sir?"

"No," I said. "You know I'm not."

"Then I must say to you, sir," he said, "what I have to say to you.

"With all possible respect, sir:" he said, "Why don't you take a flying fuck at a rolling doughnut? Why don't you take a flying fuck at the mooooooooooooon?"

I was in ecstasy.

◆◆◆

Yes, and it was during that visit here that I first learned of The Church of Jesus Christ the Kidnapped—then a tiny cult in Chicago, but destined to become the most popular American religion of all time.

It was brought to my attention by a leaflet handed to me by a clean and radiant youth, as I crossed the lobby to the staircase of my hotel.

He was jerking his head around in what then seemed an eccentric manner, as though hoping to catch someone peering out at him from behind a potted palm tree or an easy chair, or even from directly overhead, from the crystal chandelier.

He was so absorbed in firing ardent glances this way and that, that it was wholly uninteresting to him that he had just handed a leaflet to the President of the United States.

"May I ask what you're looking for, young man?" I said.

"For our Saviour, sir," he replied.

"You think He's in this hotel?" I said.

"Read the leaflet, sir," he said.

◆◆◆

So I did—in my lonely room, with the radio on.

At the very top of the leaflet was a primitive picture of Jesus, standing and with His Body facing forward, but with His Face in profile—like a one-eyed jack in a deck of playing cards.

He was gagged. He was handcuffed. One ankle was shackled and chained to a ring fixed to the floor. There was a single perfect tear dangling from the lower lid of His Eye.

Beneath the picture was a series of questions and answers, which went as follows:

QUESTION: What is your name?

ANSWER: I am the Right Reverend William Uranium-8 Wainwright, Founder of the Church of Jesus Christ the Kidnapped at 3972 Ellis Avenue, Chicago, Illinois.

QUESTION: When will God send us His Son again?

ANSWER: He already has. Jesus is here among us.

QUESTION: Why haven't we seen or heard anything about Him?

ANSWER: He has been kidnapped by the Forces of Evil.

QUESTION: What must we do?

ANSWER: We must drop whatever we are doing, and spend every waking hour in trying to find

Him. If we do not, God will exercise His Option.

QUESTION: What is God's Option?

ANSWER: He can destroy Mankind so easily, any time he chooses to.

Hi ho.

◆◆◆

I saw the young man eating alone in the diningroom that night. I marvelled that he could jerk his head around and still eat without spilling a drop. He even looked under his plate and water glass for Jesus not once, but over and over again.

I had to laugh.

◆◆◆

Chapter 39

BUT then, just when everything was going so well, when Americans were happier than they had ever been, even though the country was bankrupt and falling apart, people began to die by the millions of "The Albanian Flu" in most places, and here on Manhattan of "The Green Death."

And that was the end of the Nation. It became families, and nothing more.

Hi ho.

◆◆◆

Oh, there were claims of Dukedoms and Kingdoms and such garbage, and armies were raised and forts were built here and there. But few people admired them. They were just more bad weather and more bad gravity that families endured from time to time.

And somewhere in there a night of actual bad gravity crumbled the foundations of Machu Picchu. The condominiums and boutiques and banks and gold bricks and jewelry and pre-Columbian art collections and the Opera House and the churches, and *all* that, eloped down the Andes, wound up in the sea.

I cried.

◆◆◆

And families painted pictures everywhere of the kidnapped Jesus Christ.

◆◆◆

People continued to send news to us at the White House for a little while. We ourselves were experiencing death and death and death, and expecting to die.

Our personal hygiene deteriorated quickly. We stopped bathing and brushing our teeth regularly. The males grew beards, and let their hair grow down to their shoulders.

We began to cannibalize the White House almost absent-mindedly, burning furniture and bannisters and paneling and picture frames and so on in the fireplaces, to keep warm.

Hortense Muskellunge-13 McBundy, my personal secretary, died of flu. My valet, Edward Strawberry-4 Kleindienst, died of flu. My Vice-President, Mildred Helium-20 Theodorides, died of flu.

My science advisor, Dr. Albert Aquamarine-1 Piatigorsky, actually expired in my arms on the floor of the Oval Office.

He was almost as tall as I was. We must have been quite a sight on the floor.

"What does it all mean?" he said over and over again.

"I don't know, Albert," I said. "And maybe I'm glad I don't know."

"Ask a Chinaman!" he said, and he went to his reward, as the saying goes.

◆◆◆

Now and then the telephone would ring. It became such a rare occurrence that I took to answering it personally.

"This is your President speaking," I would say. As like as not, I would find myself talking over a tenuous, crackling circuit to some sort of mythological creature—"The King of Michigan," perhaps, or "The Emergency Governor of Florida," or "The Acting Mayor of Birmingham," or some such thing.

But there were fewer messages with each passing week. At last there were none.

I was forgotten.

Thus did my Presidency end—two thirds of the way through my second term.

And something else crucial was petering out almost as quickly—which was my irreplaceable supply of tri-benzo-Deportamil.

Hi ho.

◆◆◆

I dared not count my remaining pills until I could not help but count them, they were so few. I had become so dependent upon them, so grateful for them, that it seemed to me that my life would end when the last one was gone.

I was running out of employees, too. I was soon down to one. Everybody else had died or wandered away, since there weren't any messages any more.

The one person who remained with me was my brother, was faithful Carlos Daffodil-11 Villavicencio, the dishwasher I had embraced on my first day as a Daffodil.

◆◆◆

Chapter 40

◆◆◆◆◆◆◆◆◆◆

BECAUSE everything had dwindled so quickly, and because there was no one to behave sanely for any more, I developed a mania for counting things. I counted slats in venetian blinds. I counted the knives and forks and spoons in the kitchen. I counted the tufts of the coverlet on Abraham Lincoln's bed.

And I was counting posts in a bannister one day, on my hands and knees on the staircase, although the gravity was medium-to-light. And then I realized that a man was watching me from below.

He was dressed in buckskins and moccasins and a coon-skin hat, and carried a rifle.

"My God, President Daffodil," I said to myself, "you've really gone crazy this time. That's ol' Daniel Boone down there."

And then another man joined the first one. He was dressed like a military pilot back in the days, long before I was President, when there had been such a thing as a United States Air Force.

"Let me guess:" I said out loud, "It's either Halloween or the Fourth of July."

◆◆◆

The pilot seemed to be shocked by the condition of the White House. "What's happened here?" he said.

"All I can tell you," I said, "is that history has been made."

"This is terrible," he said.

"If you think this is bad," I told him, and I tapped my forehead with my fingertips, "you should see what it looks like in *here.*"

◆◆◆

Neither one of them even suspected that I was the President. I had become quite a mess by then.

They did not even want to talk to me, or to each other, for that matter. They were strangers, it turned out. They had simply happened to arrive at the same time—each one on an urgent mission.

They went into other rooms, and found my Sancho Panza, Carlos Daffodil-11 Villavicencio, who was making a lunch of Navy hardtack and canned

smoked oysters, and some other things he'd found.
And Carlos brought them back to me, and convinced
them that I was indeed the President of what he
called, in all sincerity, "the most powerful country in
the world."

Carlos was a really stupid man.

◆◆◆

The frontiersman had a letter for me—from the
widow in Urbana, Illinois, who had been visited a few
years before by Chinese. I had been too busy ever to
find out what the Chinese had been after out there.

"Dear Dr. Swain," it began—

"I am an undistinguished person, a piano
teacher, who is remarkable only for having been
married to a very great physicist, to have had a
beautiful son by him, and after his death, to have
been visited by a delegation of very small Chinese, one of whom said his father had known
you. His father's name was 'Fu Manchu.'

"It was the Chinese who told me about the
astonishing discovery my husband, Dr. Felix
Bauxite-13 von Peterswald, made just before he
died. My son, who is incidentally a Daffodil-11,
like yourself, and I have kept this discovery a
secret ever since, because the light it throws on
the situation of human beings in the Universe is
very demoralizing, to say the least. It has to do
with the true nature of what awaits us all after

death. What awaits us, Dr. Swain, is tedious in the extreme.

"I can't bring myself to call it 'Heaven' or 'Our Just Reward,' or any of those sweet things. All I can call it is what my husband came to call it, and what you will call it, too, after you have investigated it, which is 'The Turkey Farm.'

"In short, Dr. Swain, my husband discovered a way to talk to dead people on The Turkey Farm. He never taught the technique to me or my son, or to anybody. But the Chinese, who apparently have spies everywhere, somehow found out about it. They came to study his journals and to see what was left of his apparatus.

"After they had figured it out, they were nice enough to explain to my son and me how we might do the gruesome trick, if we wished to. They themselves were disappointed with the discovery. It was new to them, they said, but could be 'interesting only to participants in what is left of Western Civilization,' whatever that means.

"I am entrusting this letter to a friend who hopes to join a large settlement of his artificial relatives, the Berylliums, in Maryland, which is very near you.

"I address you as 'Dr. Swain' rather than 'Mr. President,' because this letter has nothing to do with the national interest. It is a highly personal letter, informing you that we have spoken to your dead sister Eliza many times on my husband's apparatus. She says that it is of the utmost importance that you come here in order that she may converse directly with you.

"We eagerly await your visit. Please do not be insulted by the behavior of my son and your brother, David Daffodil-11 von Peterswald, who cannot prevent himself from speaking obscenities and making insulting gestures at even the most inappropriate moments. He is a victim of Tourette's Disease.

"Your faithful servant,
"Wilma Pachysandra-17 von Peterswald."

Hi ho

◆◆◆

Chapter 41

I was deeply moved, despite tri-benzo-Deportamil.

I stared out at the frontiersman's sweaty horse, which was grazing in the high grass of the White House lawn. And then I turned to the messenger himself. "How came you by this message?" I said.

He told me that he had accidentally shot a man, apparently Wilma Pachysandra-17 von Peterswald's friend, the Beryllium, on the border between Tennessee and West Virginia. He had mistaken him for an hereditary enemy.

"I thought he was Newton McCoy," he said.

He tried to nurse his innocent victim back to

health, but he died of gangrene. But, before he died, the Beryllium made him promise as a Christian to deliver a letter he had himself sworn to hand over to the President of the United States.

◆◆◆

I asked him his name.

"Byron Hatfield," he said.

"What is your Government-issue middle name?" I said.

"We never paid no mind to that," he replied.

It turned out that he belonged to one of the few genuine extended families of blood relatives in the country, which had been at perpetual war with another such family since 1882.

"We never was big for them new-fangled middle names," he said.

◆◆◆

The frontiersman and I were seated on spindly golden ballroom chairs which had supposedly been bought for the White House by Jacqueline Kennedy so long ago. The pilot was similarly supported, alertly awaiting his turn to speak. I glanced at the name-plate over the breast pocket of the pilot. It said this:

CAPT. BERNARD O'HARE

◆◆◆

"Captain," I said, "you're another one who doesn't seem to go in for the new-fangled middle names." I noticed, too, that he was much too old to be only a captain, even if there had still been such a thing. He was in fact almost sixty.

I concluded that he was a lunatic who had found the costume somewhere. I supposed that he had become so elated and addled by his new appearance, that nothing would do but that he show himself off to his President.

The truth was, though, that he was perfectly sane. He had been stationed for the past eleven years in the bottom of a secret, underground silo in Rock Creek Park. I had never heard of the silo before.

But there was a Presidential helicopter concealed in it, along with thousands of gallons of absolutely priceless gasoline.

◆◆◆

He had come out at last, in violation of his orders, he said, to find out "what on Earth was going on."

I had to laugh.

◆◆◆

"Is the helicopter still ready to fly?" I asked.

"Yes, sir, it is," he said. He had been maintaining it single-handedly for the past two years. His mechanics had wandered off one-by-one.

"Young man," I said, "I'm going to give you a

medal for this." I took a button from my own tattered lapel, and I pinned it to his.

It said this, of course:

◆◆◆

Chapter 42

✦✦✦✦✦✦✦✦✦

THE frontiersman refused a similar decoration. He asked for food, instead —to sustain him on his long trip back to his native mountains.

We gave him what we had, which was all the hardtack and canned smoked oysters his saddlebags would hold.

✦✦✦

Yes, and Captain Bernard O'Hare and Carlos Daffodil-11 Villavicencio and I took off from the silo on the following dawn. It was a day of such salubrious gravity, that our helicopter expended no more energy than would have an airborne milkweed seed.

As we fluttered over the White House, I waved to it.

"Goodbye," I said.

◆◆◆

My plan was to fly first to Indianapolis, which had become densely populated with Daffodils. They had been flocking there from everywhere.

We would leave Carlos there, to be cared for by his artificial relatives during his sunset years. I was glad to be getting rid of him. He bored me to tears.

◆◆◆

We would go next to Urbana, I told Captain O'Hare —and then to my childhood home in Vermont.

"After that," I promised, "the helicopter is yours, Captain. You can fly like a bird wherever you wish. But you're going to have a rotten time of it, if you don't give yourself a good middle name."

"You're the President," he said. "You give me a name."

"I dub thee 'Eagle-1,'" I said.

He was awfully pleased. He loved the medal, too.

◆◆◆

Yes, and I still had a little tri-benzo-Deportamil left, and I was so delighted to be going simply anywhere, after having been cooped up in Washington, D.C. so long, that I heard myself singing for the first time in years.

I remember the song I sang, too. It was one Eliza

and I used to sing a lot in secret, back when we were still believed to be idiots. We would sing it where nobody could hear us—in the mausoleum of Professor Elihu Roosevelt Swain.

And I think now that I will teach it to Melody and Isadore at my birthday party. It is such a good song for them to sing when they set out for new adventures on the Island of Death.

It goes like this:

"Oh, we're off to see the Wizard,
"The wonderful Wizard of Oz.

***

"If ever a whiz of a Wiz there was,
"It was the Wizard of Oz."*

◆◆◆

And so on.

◆◆◆

Hi ho.

◆◆◆

Chapter 43

◆◆◆◆◆◆◆◆◆◆◆

ELODY and Isadore went down to Wall Street today—to visit Isadore's large family, the Raspberries. I was invited to become a Raspberry at one time. So was Vera Chipmunk-5 Zappa. We both declined.

Yes, and I took a walk of my own—up to the baby's pyramid at Broadway and Forty-second, then across Forty-third Street to the old Daffodil Club, to what had been the Century Association before that; and then eastward across Forty-eighth Street to the townhouse which was slave quarters for Vera's farm, which at one time had been my parent's home.

I encountered Vera herself on the steps of the

townhouse. Her slaves were all over in what used to be United Nations Park, planting watermelons and corn and sunflowers. I could hear them singing "Ol' Man River." They were so happy all the time. They considered themselves very lucky to be slaves.

They were all Chipmunk-5's, and about two-thirds of them were former Raspberries. People who wished to become slaves of Vera had to change their middle names to Chipmunk-5.

Hi ho.

◆◆◆

Vera usually labored right along with her slaves. She loved hard work. But now I caught her tinkering idly with a beautiful Zeiss microscope, which one of her slaves had unearthed in the ruins of a hospital only the day before. It had been protected all through the years by its original factory packing case.

Vera had not sensed my approach. She was peering into the instrument and turning knobs with childlike seriousness and ineptitude. It was obvious that she had never used a microscope before.

I stole closer to her, and then I said, "Boo!"

She jerked her head away from the eyepiece.

"Hello," I said.

"You scared me to death," she said.

"Sorry," I said, and I laughed.

These ancient games go on and on. It's nice they do.

✦✦✦

"I can't see anything," she said. She was complaining about the microscope.

"Just squiggly little animals that want to kill and eat us," I said. "You really want to see those?"

"I was looking at an opal," she said. She had draped an opal and diamond bracelet over the stage of the microscope. She had a collection of precious stones which would have been worth millions of dollars in olden times. People gave her all the jewels they found, just as they gave me all the candlesticks.

✦✦✦

Jewels were useless. So were candlesticks, since there weren't such things on Manhattan as candles any more. People lit their homes at night with burning rags stuck in bowls of animal fat.

"There's probably Green Death on the opal," I said. "There's probably Green Death on everything."

The reason that we ourselves did not die of The Green Death, by the way, was that we took an antidote which was discovered by accident by Isadore's family, the Raspberries.

We had only to withhold the antidote from a troublemaker, or from an army of troublemakers, for that matter, and he or she or they would be exiled quickly to the afterlife, to The Turkey Farm.

✦✦✦

There weren't any great scientists among the Raspberries, incidentally. They discovered the antidote through dumb luck. They ate fish without cleaning them, and the antidote, probably pollution left over from olden times, was somewhere in the guts of the fish they ate.

◆◆◆

"Vera," I said, "if you ever got that microscope to work, you would see something that would break your heart."

"What would break my heart?" she said.

"You'd see the organisms that cause The Green Death," I said.

"Why would that make me cry?" she said.

"Because you're a woman of conscience," I said. "Don't you realize that we kill them by the *trillions* —every time we take our antidote?"

I laughed.

She did not laugh.

"The reason I am not laughing," she said, "is that you, coming along so unexpectedly, have spoiled a surprise for your birthday."

"How is that?" I said.

She spoke of one of her slaves. "Donna was going to make a present of this to you. Now you won't be surprised."

"Um," I said.

"She thought it was an extra-fancy kind of candlestick."

◆◆◆

She confided to me that Melody and Isadore had paid her a call earlier in the week, had told her again how much they hoped to be her slaves someday.

"I tried to tell 'em that slavery wasn't for everybody," she said.

◆◆◆

"Answer me this," she went on, "What happens to all my slaves when I die?"

" 'Take no thought for the morrow,' " I told her, " 'for the morrow shall take thought for the things of itself. Sufficient unto the day is the evil thereof.'

"Amen," I said.

◆◆◆

Chapter 44

◆◆◆◆◆◆◆◆◆◆

OLD Vera and I reminisced there on the townhouse steps about the Battle of Lake Maxinkuckee, in northern Indiana. I had seen it from a helicopter on my way to Urbana. Vera had been in the actual thick of it with her alcoholic husband, Lee Razorclam-13 Zappa. They were cooks in one of the King of Michigan's field kitchens on the ground below.

"You all looked like ants to me down there," I said, "or like germs under a microscope." We didn't dare come down close, for fear of being shot.

"That's what we felt like, too," she said.

"If I had known you then, I would have tried to rescue you," I said.

"That would have been like trying to rescue a germ from a million other germs, Wilbur," she said.

◆◆◆

Not only did Vera have to put up with shells and bullets whistling over the kitchen tent. She had to defend herself against her husband, too, who was drunk. He beat her up in the midst of battle.

He blacked both her eyes and broke her jaw. He threw her out through the tent flaps. She landed on her back in the mud. Then he came out to explain to her how she could avoid similar beatings in the future.

He came out just in time to be skewered by the lance of an enemy cavalryman.

"And what's the moral of that story, do you think?" I asked her.

She lay a callused palm on my knee. "Wilbur—don't ever get married," she replied.

◆◆◆

We talked some about Indianapolis, which I had seen on the same trip, and where she and her husband had been a waitress and a bartender for a Thirteen Club —before they joined the army of the King of Michigan.

I asked her what the club was like inside.

"Oh, you know—" she said, "they had stuffed black cats and jack-o-lanterns, and aces of spades stuck to the tables with daggers and all. I used to wear net stockings and spike heels and a mask and all. All the waitresses and the bartenders and the bouncer wore vampire fangs."

"Um," I said.

"We used to call our hamburgers 'Batburgers,'" she said.

"Uh huh," I said.

"We used to call tomato juice with a shot of gin a 'Dracula's Delight,'" she said.

"Right," I said.

"It was just like a Thirteen Club anywhere," she said, "but it never went over. Indianapolis just wasn't a big Thirteen town, even though there were plenty of Thirteens there. It was a Daffodil town. You weren't anything if you weren't a Daffodil."

◆◆◆

Chapter 45

✦✦✦✦✦✦✦✦✦✦✦

I tell you—I have been
regaled as a multimillionaire, as a pediatrician, as a
Senator, and as a President. But nothing can match
for sincerity the welcome Indianapolis, Indiana, gave
me as a Daffodil!

The people there were poor, and had suffered an
awful lot of death, and all the public services had
broken down, and they were worried about battles
raging not far away. But they put on parades and
feasts for me, and for Carlos Daffodil-11 Villavicencio, too, of course, which would have blinded
ancient Rome.

✦✦✦

Captain Bernard Eagle-1 O'Hare said to me, "My gosh, Mr. President—if I'd known about this, I would have asked you to make me a Daffodil."

So I said, "I hereby dub thee a Daffodil."

✦✦✦

But the most satisfying and educational thing I saw out there was a weekly family meeting of Daffodils.

Yes, and I got to vote at that meeting, and so did my pilot, and so did Carlos, and so did every man, woman, and every child over the age of nine.

With a little luck, I might even have become Chairperson of the meeting, although I had been in town for less than a day. The Chairperson was chosen by lot from all assembled. And the winner of the drawing that night was an eleven-year-old black girl named Dorothy Daffodil-7 Garland.

She was fully prepared to run the meeting, and so, I suppose, was every person there.

✦✦✦

She marched up to the lectern, which was nearly as tall as she was.

That little cousin of mine stood on a chair, without any apologies or self-mockery. She banged the meeting to order with a yellow gavel, and she told her silenced and respectful relatives, "The President of the United States is present, as most of you know.

With your permission, I will ask him to say a few words to us at the conclusion of our regular business.

"Will somebody put that in the form of a motion?" she said.

"I move that Cousin Wilbur be asked to address the meeting at the conclusion of regular business," said an old man sitting next to me.

This was seconded and put to a voice vote.

The motion carried, but with a scattering of seemingly heartfelt, by-no-means joshing, "Nays" and "Noes."

Hi ho.

◆◆◆

The most pressing business had to do with selecting four replacements for fallen Daffodils in the army of the King of Michigan, who was at war simultaneously with Great Lakes pirates and the Duke of Oklahoma.

There was one strapping young man, I remember, a blacksmith, in fact, who told the meeting, "Send me. There's nothing I'd rather do than kill me some 'Sooners,' long as they ain't Daffodils." And so on.

To my surprise, he was scolded by several speakers for his military ardor. He was told that war wasn't supposed to be fun, and in fact wasn't fun—that tragedy was being discussed, and that he had better put on a tragic face, or he would be ejected from the meeting.

"Sooners" were people from Oklahoma, and, by extension, anybody in the service of the Duke of

Oklahoma, which included "Show Me's" from Missouri and "Jayhawkers" from Kansas and "Hawkeyes" from Iowa, and on and on.

The blacksmith was told that "Sooners" were human beings, too, no better or worse than "Hoosiers," who were people from Indiana.

And the old man who had moved that I be allowed to speak later on got up and said this: "Young man, you're no better than the Albanian influenza or The Green Death, if you can kill for joy."

♦♦♦

I was impressed. I realized that nations could never acknowledge their own wars as tragedies, but that families not only could but had to.

Bully for them!

♦♦♦

The chief reason the blacksmith was not allowed to go to war, though, was that he had so far fathered three illegitimate children by different women, "and had two more in the oven," as someone said.

He wasn't going to be allowed to run away from caring for all those babies.

♦♦♦

Chapter 46

Even the children and the drunks and the lunatics at that meeting seemed shrewdly familiar with parliamentary procedures. The little girl behind the lectern kept things moving so briskly and purposefully that she might have been some sort of goddess up there, equipped with an armload of thunderbolts.

I was so filled with respect for these procedures, which had always seemed like such solemn tomfoolery to me before.

◆◆◆

And I am still so respectful, that I have just looked up their inventor in my Encyclopædia here in the Empire State Building.

His name was Henry Martyn Robert. He was a graduate of West Point. He was an engineer. He became a general by and by. But, just before the Civil War, when he was a lieutenant stationed in New Bedford, Massachusetts, he had to run a church meeting, and he lost control of it.

There were no rules.

So this soldier sat down and wrote some rules, which were the identical rules I saw followed in Indianapolis. They were published as *Robert's Rules of Order*, which I now believe to be one of the four greatest inventions by Americans.

The other three, in my opinion, were The Bill of Rights, the principles of Alcoholics Anonymous, and the artificial extended families envisioned by Eliza and me.

◆◆◆

The three recruits which the Indianapolis Daffodils finally voted to send off to the King of Michigan, incidentally, were all people who could be most easily spared, and who, in the opinion of the voters, had had the most carefree lives so far.

Hi ho.

◆◆◆

The next order of business had to do with feeding and sheltering Daffodil refugees, who were trickling into town from all the fighting in the northern part of the state.

The meeting again discouraged an enthusiast. A young woman, quite beautiful but disorderly, and clearly crazed by altruism, said that she could take at least twenty refugees into her home.

Somebody else got up and said to her that she was such an incompetent housekeeper that her own children had gone to live with other relatives.

Another person pointed out to her that she was so absent-minded that her dog would have starved to death, if it weren't for neighbors, and that she had accidentally set fire to her house three times.

◆◆◆

This sounds as though the people at the meeting were being cruel. But they all called her "Cousin Grace" or "Sister Grace," as the case might be. She was my cousin too, of course. She was a Daffodil-13.

What was more: She was a menace only to herself, so nobody was particularly mad at her. Her children had wandered off to better-run houses almost as soon as they were able to walk, I was told. That was surely one of the most attractive features of Eliza's and my invention, I think: Children had so many homes and parents to choose from.

Cousin Grace, for her part, heard all the bad reports on herself as though they were surprising to her, but no doubt true. She did not flee in tears. She stayed for the rest of the meeting, obeying Robert's Rules of Order, and looking sympathetic and alert.

At one point, under "New Business," Cousin Grace made a motion that any Daffodil who served with the Great Lakes Pirates or in the army of the Duke of Oklahoma should be expelled from the family.

Nobody would second this.

And the little girl running the meeting told her, "Cousin Grace, you know as well as anybody here, 'Once a Daffodil, always a Daffodil.'"

◆◆◆

Chapter 47

◆◆◆◆◆◆◆◆◆

IT was at last my turn to speak.

"Brothers and Sisters and Cousins—" I said, "your nation has wasted away. As you can see, your President has also become a shadow of his former shadow. You have nobody but your doddering Cousin Wilbur here."

"You were a damn good President, Brother Billy," somebody called from the back of the room.

"I would have liked to give my country peace as well as brotherhood and sisterhood," I went on. "There is no peace, I'm sorry to say. We find it. We lose it. We find it again. We lose it again. Thank God, at least, that the machines have decided not to fight any more. It's just people now.

"And thank God that there's no such thing as a battle between strangers any more. I don't care who fights who—everybody will have relatives on the other side."

◆◆◆

Most of the people at the meeting were not only *Daffodils*, but also searchers for the kidnapped Jesus. It was a disconcerting sort of audience to address, I found. No matter what I said, they kept jerking their heads this way and that, hoping to catch sight of Jesus.

But I seemed to be getting across, for they applauded or cheered at appropriate moments—so I pressed on.

◆◆◆

"Because we're just families, and not a nation any more," I said, "it's much easier for us to give and receive mercy in war."

"I have just come from observing a battle far to the north of here, in the region of Lake Maxinkuckee. It was horses and spears and rifles and knives and pistols, and a cannon or two. I saw several people killed. I also saw many people embracing, and there seemed to be a great deal of deserting and surrendering going on.

"This much news I can bring you from the Battle of Lake Maxinkuckee:" I said—
"It is no massacre."

◆◆◆

Chapter 48

◆◆◆◆◆◆◆◆◆◆

WHILE in Indianapolis, I received an invitation by radio from the King of Michigan. It was Napoleonic in tone. It said that the King would be pleased "to hold an audience for the President of the United States in his Summer Palace on Lake Maxinkuckee." It said that his sentinels had been instructed to grant me safe passage. It said that the battle was over. "Victory is ours," it said.

So my pilot and I flew there.

We left my faithful servant, Carlos Daffodil-11 Villavicencio, to spend his declining years among his countless relatives.

"Good luck, Brother Carlos," I said.

"Home at last, Meester President, me Brudder,"

he replied. "Tanks you and tanks God for everything. Lonesome no more!"

◆◆◆

My meeting with the King of Michigan would have been called an "historic occasion" in olden times. There would have been cameras and microphones and reporters there. As it was, there were notetakers there, whom the King called his "scribes."

And he was right to give those people with pens and paper that archaic title. Most of his soldiers could scarcely read or write.

◆◆◆

Captain O'Hare and I landed on the manicured lawn before the King's Summer Palace, which had been a private military academy at one time. Soldiers, who had behaved badly in the recent battle, I suppose, were on their knees everywhere, guarded by military policemen. They were cutting grass with bayonets and pocket knives and scissors—as a punishment.

◆◆◆

Captain O'Hare and I entered the palace between two lines of soldiers. They were an honor guard of some sort, I suppose. Each one held aloft a banner, which was embroidered with the totem of his artificial extended family—an apple, an alligator, the chemical symbol for lithium, and so on.

It was such a comically trite historical situation, I

thought. Aside from battles, the history of nations seemed to consist of nothing but powerless old poops like myself, heavily medicated and vaguely beloved in the long ago, coming to kiss the boots of young psychopaths.

Inside myself, I had to laugh.

◆◆◆

I was ushered alone into the King's spartan private quarters. It was a huge room, where the military academy must have held dances at one time. Now there was only a folding cot in there, a long table covered with maps, and a stack of folding chairs against one wall.

The King himself sat at the map table, ostentatiously reading a book, which turned out to be Thucydides' *History of the Peloponnesian War.*

Behind him, standing, were three male scribes—with pencils and pads.

There was no place for me or anyone else to sit.

I positioned myself before him, my mouldy Homburg in hand. He did not look up from his book immediately, although the doorkeeper had certainly announced me loudly enough.

"Your Majesty," the doorkeeper had said, "Dr. Wilbur Daffodil-11 Swain, the President of the United States!!"

◆◆◆

He looked up at last, and I was amused to see that he was the spit and image of his grandfather, Dr. Stewart Rawlings Mott, the physician who had looked after my sister and me in Vermont so long ago.

◆◆◆

I was not in the least afraid of him. Tri-benzo-Deportamil was making me soigné and blasé, of course. But, also, I had had more than enough of the low comedy of living by then. I would have found it a rather shapely adventure, if the King had elected to hustle me in front of a firing squad.

"We thought you were dead," he said.

"No, your Majesty," I said.

"It's been so long since we heard anything about you," he said.

"Washington, D.C., runs out of ideas from time to time," I said.

◆◆◆

The scribes were taking all this down, all this history that was being made.

He held up the spine of the book so I could read it. "Thucydides," he said.

"Um," I said.

"History is all I read," he said.

"That is wise for a man in your position, your Majesty," I replied.

"Those who fail to learn from history are condemned to repeat it," he said.

The scribes scribbled away.

"Yes," I said. "If our descendents don't study our times closely, they will find that they have again exhausted the planet's fossil fuels, that they have again died by the millions of influenza and The Green Death, that the sky has again been turned yellow by the propellants for underarm deodorants, that they have again elected a senile President two meters tall, and that they are yet again the intellectual and spiritual inferiors of teeny-weeny Chinese."

He did not join my laughter.

I addressed his scribes directly, speaking over his head. "History is merely a list of surprises," I said. "It can only prepare us to be surprised yet again. Please write that down."

◆◆◆

Chapter 49

◆◆◆◆◆◆◆◆◆◆◆

IT turned out that the young King had an historic document he wished me to sign. It was brief. In it, I acknowledged that I, the President of the United States of America, no longer exercised any control over that part of the North American Continent which was sold by Napoleon Bonaparte to my country in 1803, and which was known as "The Louisiana Purchase."

I, therefore, according to the document, sold it for a dollar, to Stewart Oriole-2 Mott, the King of Michigan.

I signed with the teeny-weeniest signature possible. It looked like a baby ant. "Enjoy it in good health!" I said.

The territory I had sold him was largely occupied by the Duke of Oklahoma, and, no doubt, by other potentates and panjandrums unknown to me.

After that, we chatted some about his grandfather.

Then Captain O'Hare and I took off for Urbana, Illinois, and an electronic reunion with my sister, who had been dead so long.

Hi ho.

◆◆◆

Yes, and I write now with a palsied hand and an aching head, for I drank much too much at my birthday party last night.

Vera Chipmunk-5 Zappa arrived encrusted with diamonds, borne through the ailanthus forest in a sedan chair, accompanied by an entourage of fourteen slaves. She brought me wine and beer, which made me drunk. But her most intoxicating gifts were a thousand candles she and her slaves had made in a colonial candle mold. We fitted them into the empty mouths of my thousand candlesticks, and deployed them over the lobby floor.

Then we lit them all.

Standing among all those tiny, wavering lights, I felt as though I were God, up to my knees in the Milky Way.

◆◆◆

Epilogue

DR. Swain died before he could write any more. He went to his just reward.

There was nobody to read what he had written anyway—to complain about all the loose ends of the yarn he had spun.

He had reached the climax of his story, at any rate, with his reselling of the Louisiana Purchase to a bandit chief—for a dollar he never received.

Yes, and he died proud of what he and his sister had done to reform their society, for he left this poem, perhaps hoping that someone would use it for his epitaph:

"And how did we then face the odds,
"Of man's rude slapstick, yes, and God's?
"Quite at home and unafraid,
"Thank you,
"In a game our dreams remade."

◆◆◆

He never got to tell about the electronic device in Urbana, which made it possible for him to reunite his mind with that of his dead sister, to recreate the genius they had been in childhood.

The device, which those few people who knew about it called "The Hooligan," consisted of a seemingly ordinary length of brown clay pipe—two meters long and twenty centimeters in diameter. It was placed just so—atop a steel cabinet containing controls for a huge particle-accelerator. The particle-accelerator was a tubular magnetic race track for subatomic entities which looped through cornfields on the edge of town.

Yes.

And the Hooligan was itself a ghost, in a way, since the particle-accelerator had been dead for a long time, for want of electricity, for want of enthusiasts for all it could do.

A janitor, Francis Iron-7 Hooligan, stored the piece of pipe atop the dead cabinet, rested his lunchpail there, too, for the moment. He heard voices from the pipe.

230

◆◆◆

He fetched the scientist whose apparatus this had been, Dr. Felix Bauxite-13 von Peterswald. But the pipe refused to talk again.

Dr. von Peterswald demonstrated that he was a great scientist, however, with his willingness to believe the ignorant Mr. Hooligan. He made the janitor go over his story again and again.

"The lunchpail," he said at last. "Where is your lunchpail?"

Hooligan had it in his hand.

Dr. von Peterswald instructed him to place it in relation to the pipe exactly as it had been before.

The pipe began promptly to talk again.

◆◆◆

The talkers identified themselves as persons in the afterlife. They were backed by a demoralized chorus of persons who complained to each other of tedium and social slights and minor ailments, and so on.

As Dr. von Peterswald said in his secret diary: "It sounded like nothing so much as the other end of a telephone call on a rainy autumn day—to a badly run turkey farm."

Hi ho.

◆◆◆

When Dr. Swain talked to his sister Eliza over the Hooligan, he was in the company of the widow of Dr.

von Peterswald, Wilma Pachysandra-17 von Peterswald, and her fifteen-year-old son, David Daffodil-11 von Peterswald, a brother of Dr. Swain, and a victim of Tourette's Disease.

◆◆◆

Poor David suffered an attack of his disease—just as Dr. Swain was beginning to talk with Eliza across the Great Divide.

David tried to choke down the involuntary stream of obscenities, but succeeded only in raising their pitch an octave. "Shit . . . sputum . . . scrotum . . . cloaca . . . asshole . . . pecker . . . mucous membrane . . . earwax . . . piss," he said.

◆◆◆

And Dr. Swain himself went out of control. He climbed involuntarily on top of the cabinet, as tall and old as he was. He crouched over the pipe, to be that much closer to his sister. He hung his head upside-down in front of the business end of the pipe, and knocked the crucial lunchpail to the floor, breaking the connection.

"Hello? Hello?" he said.

"Perineum . . . fuck . . . turd . . . glans . . . mount of Venus . . . afterbirth," said the boy.

◆◆◆

The widow von Peterswald was the only stable person on the Urbana end, so it was she who re-

stored the lunchpail to its correct position. She
had to jam it rather brutally between the pipe and
the knee of the President. Then she found herself
trapped in a grotesque position, bent at a right an-
gle across the top of the cabinet, one arm extended, and her feet a few inches off the floor.
The President had clamped down not only on the
lunchpail, but on her hand.

"Hello? Hello?" said the President, his head upside
down.

◆◆◆

There were answering gabblings and gobblings and
squawks and clucks from the other end.

Somebody sneezed.

"Bugger . . . defecate . . . semen . . . balls," said the
boy.

◆◆◆

Before Eliza could speak again, dead people in the
background sensed that poor David was a kindred
spirit, as outraged by the human condition in the
Universe as they were. So they egged him on, and
contributed obscenities of their own.

"You tell 'em, kid," they said, and so on.

And they doubled everything. "Double cock! Double clit!" they'd say. "Double shit!" and so on.

It was bedlam.

◆◆◆

But Dr. Swain and his sister got together anyway, with such convulsive intimacy that Dr. Swain would have crawled into the pipe, if he could.

Yes, and what Eliza wanted from him was that he should die as soon as possible, so that the two of them could put their heads together. She wanted then to figure out ways to improve the utterly unsatisfactory, so-called "Paradise."

◆◆◆

"Are you being tortured there?" he asked her.

"No," she said, "we are being bored stiff. Whoever designed this place knew nothing about human beings. Please, brother Wilbur," she said, "this is *Eternity* here. This is *forever!* Where you are now is just nothing in terms of time! It's a joke! Blow your brains out as quick as you can."

And so on.

◆◆◆

Dr. Swain told her about the problems the living had been having with incurable diseases. The two of them, thinking as one, made child's play of the mystery.

The explanation was this: The flu germs were Martians, whose invasion had apparently been repelled by anti-bodies in the systems of the survivors, since, for the moment, anyway, there was no more flu.

The Green Death, on the other hand, was caused by microscopic Chinese, who were peace-loving and meant no one any harm. They were nonetheless invariably fatal to normal-sized human beings when inhaled or ingested.

And so on.

◆◆◆

Dr. Swain asked his sister what sort of communications apparatus there was on the other end—whether Eliza, too, was squatting over a piece of pipe, or what.

Eliza told him that there was no apparatus, but only a feeling.

"What is the feeling?" he said.

"You would have to be dead to understand my description of it," she said.

"Try it anyway, Eliza," he said.

"It is like being dead," she said.

"A feeling of deadness," he said tentatively, trying to understand.

"Yes—coldness and clamminess—" she said.

"Um," he said.

"But also like being surrounded by a swarm of invisible bees," she said. "Your voice comes from the bees."

Hi ho.

◆◆◆

When Dr. Swain was through with this particular ordeal, he had only eleven tablets left of tri-benzo-Deportamil, which were originally created, of course, not as a narcotic for presidents, but as suppressants for the symptoms of Tourette's Disease.

And the remaining pills, when he displayed them to himself in the palm of his huge hand, inevitably looked to him like the remaining grains in the hourglass of his life.

◆◆◆

Dr. Swain was standing in the sunshine outside the laboratory building containing the Hooligan. With him were the widow and her son. The widow had the lunchpail, so that only she could turn the Hooligan on.

The gravity was light. Dr. Swain had an erection. So did the boy. So did Captain Bernard Daffodil-11 O'Hare, who stood by the helicopter nearby.

Presumably, the erectile tissues in the widow's body were also engorged.

"You know what you looked like on top of that cabinet, Mr. President?" said the boy. He was clearly sickened by what his disease was about to make him say.

"No," said Dr. Swain.

"Like the biggest baboon in the world—trying to fuck a football," blurted the boy.

Dr. Swain, in order to avoid any more insults like that, handed his remaining supply of tri-benzo-Deportamil to the boy.

◆◆◆

The consequences of his withdrawal from tri-benzo-Deportamil were spectacular. Dr. Swain had to be tied to a bed in the widow's house for six nights and days.

Somewhere in there he made love to the widow, conceiving a son who would become the father of Melody Oriole-2 von Peterswald.

Yes, and somewhere in there the widow passed on to him what she had learned from the Chinese—that they had become successful manipulators of the Universe by combining harmonious minds.

◆◆◆

Yes, and then he had his pilot fly him to Manhattan, the Island of Death. He intended to die there, to join his sister in the afterlife—as a result of inhaling and ingesting invisible Chinese communists.

Captain O'Hare, not wishing to die yet himself, lowered his President by means of a winch and rope and harness to the observation deck of the Empire State Building.

The President spent the remainder of the day up there, enjoying the view. And then, breathing deeply with every few steps, hoping to inhale Chinese communists, he descended the stairs.

It was twilight when he reached the bottom.

◆◆◆

There were human skeletons in the lobby—in rotting nests of rags. The walls were zebra-striped with soot from cooking fires of long ago.

There was a painting of Jesus Christ the Kidnapped on one wall.

Dr. Swain for the first time heard the shuddering whir of bats leaving the subway system for the night.

He considered himself to be already a dead man— a brother to the skeletons.

But six members of the Raspberry family, who had observed his arrival by helicopter, suddenly came out of hiding in the lobby. They were armed with spears and knives.

◆◆◆

When they understood who they had captured, they were thrilled. He was a treasure to them not because he was President, but because he had been to medical school.

"A doctor! Now we have everything!" said one.

Yes, and they would not hear of his wish to die. They forced him to swallow a small trapezoid of what seemed to be a tasteless sort of peanut-brittle. It was in fact boiled and dried fish guts, which contained the antidote to The Green Death.

Hi ho.

◆◆◆

The Raspberries hustled him down to the Financial District at once, for Hiroshi Raspberry-20 Yamashiro, the head of the family, was deathly ill.

◆◆◆

The man seemed to have pneumonia. Dr. Swain could do nothing for him but what physicians of a century before would have done, which was to keep his body warm and his forehead cool—and to wait.

Either the fever would break, or the man would die.

◆◆◆

The fever broke.

As a reward, the Raspberries brought their most precious possessions to Dr. Swain on the floor of the New York Stock Exchange. There was a clock-radio, an alto saxophone, a fully-fitted toiletries kit, a model of the Eiffel Tower with a thermometer in it—and on and on.

From all this junk, and merely to be polite, Dr. Swain selected a single brass candlestick.

And thus was the legend established that he was crazy about candlesticks.

Thereafter, everybody would give him candlesticks.

◆◆◆

He did not like the communal life of the Raspberries, which required him, among other things, to jerk his head around perpetually, in search of the kidnapped Jesus Christ.

So he cleaned up the lobby of the Empire State Building, and moved in there. The Raspberries supplied him with food.

And time flew.

◆◆◆

Somewhere in there, Vera Chipmunk-5 Zappa arrived, and was given the antidote by the Raspberries. They hoped she would be Dr. Swain's nurse.

And she was his nurse for a little while, but then she started her model farm.

◆◆◆

And little Melody arrived a long time after that, pregnant, and pushing her pathetic worldly goods ahead of her in a dilapidated baby carriage. Among those goods was a Dresden candlestick. Even in the Kingdom of Michigan, it was well known that the legendary King of New York was crazy about candlesticks.

Melody's candlestick depicted a nobleman's flirtation with a shepherdess at the foot of a treetrunk enlaced in flowering vines.

Melody's candlestick was broken on the old man's last birthday. It was kicked over by Wanda Chipmunk-5 Rivera, an intoxicated slave.

◆◆◆

When Melody first presented herself at the Empire State Building, and Dr. Swain came out to ask who she was and what she wanted, she went down on her knees to him. Her little hands were extended before her, holding the candlestick.

"Hello, Grandfather," she said.

He hesitated for a moment. But then he helped her to her feet. "Come in," he said. "Come in, come in."

◆◆◆

Dr. Swain did not know at that time that he had sired a son during his withdrawal from tri-benzo-Deportamil in Urbana. He supposed that Melody was a random supplicant and fan. Nor did he bring to that first encounter any daydreams of having descendents somewhere. He had never much wanted to reproduce himself.

So, when Melody gave him shy but convincing arguments that she was an actual blood relative, he had a feeling that he, as he later explained to Vera Chipmunk-5 Zappa, " had somehow sprung a huge leak. And out of that sudden, painless opening," he went on, "there crawled a famished child, pregnant and clasping a Dresden candlestick.

"Hi ho."

◆◆◆

Melody's story was this:

Her father, who was the illegitimate child of Dr. Swain and the widow in Urbana, was one of the few survivors of the so-called "Urbana Massacre." He was then pressed into service as a drummer boy in the army of the perpetrator of the massacre, the Duke of Oklahoma.

The boy begat Melody at the age of fourteen. Her

mother was a forty-year-old laundress who had attached herself to the army. Melody was given the middle name "Oriole-2", to ensure that she would be treated with maximal mercy, should she be captured by the forces of Stewart Oriole-2 Mott, the King of Michigan, the chief enemy of the Duke.

And she was in fact captured when a six-year-old —after the Battle of Iowa City, in which her father and mother were slain.

Hi ho.

◆◆◆

Yes, and the King of Michigan had become so decadent by then, that he maintained a seraglio of captured children with the same middle name as his— which, of course, was Oriole-2. Little Melody was added to that pitiful zoo.

But, as her ordeals became more disgusting, so did she gain increasing inner strength from her father's dying words to her, which were these:

"You are a princess. You are the granddaughter of the King of Candlesticks, of the King of New York."

Hi ho.

◆◆◆

And then, one night, she stole the Dresden candlestick from the tent of the sleeping King.

Then Melody crawled under the flaps of the tent and into the moonlit world outside.

◆◆◆

Thus began her incredible journey eastward, ever eastward, in search of her legendary grandfather. His palace was one of the tallest buildings in the world.

She would encounter relatives everywhere—if not Orioles, then at least birds or living things of some kind.

They would feed her and point the way.

One would give her a raincoat. Another would give her a sweater and a magnetic compass. Another would give her a baby carriage. Another would give her an alarm clock.

Another would give her a needle and thread, and a gold thimble, too.

Another would row her across the Harlem River to the Island of Death, at the risk of his own life.

And so on.

–Das Ende–

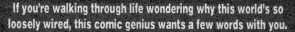